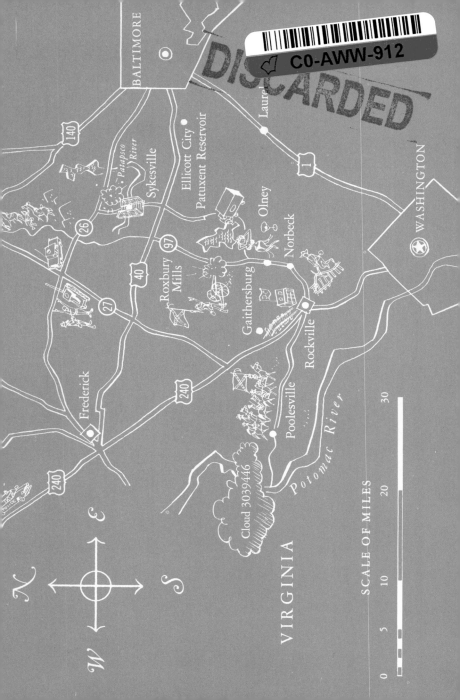

BALTIMORE

140

Patapsco River

Sykesville

Ellicott City

Laurel

1

WASHINGTON

Olney

Patuxent Reservoir

Norbeck

26

97

40

Roxbury Mills

Gaithersburg

27

Rockville

Frederick

240

Poolesville

Potomac River

240

Cloud 3039446

VIRGINIA

N

E

S

W

SCALE OF MILES

0   5   10   20   30

```
E        Love,
647        An end to bugling
.L85
```

AN END TO BUGLING

An
End
to
Bugling

EDMUND G. LOVE

ILLUSTRATED BY BOB BUGG

HARPER & ROW, PUBLISHERS
NEW YORK, EVANSTON, AND LONDON

FIRST EDITION

A-N

LIBRARY OF CONGRESS CATALOG CARD NUMBER: 63-10612

To Blanche

AN END TO BUGLING

HEADQUARTERS
SUPREME COMMAND, ALL ARMIES

27 June, 1963

TO: COMMANDING GENERAL, CAVALRY, ARMY OF NORTHERN VIRGINIA
SUBJECT: LETTER ORDERS—DEMONSTRATION EXERCISE, 63–235

1. The Supreme Commander has decided to join in the commemoration of the centennial of the American Civil War. Pursuant to these orders, therefore, the Cavalry of the Army of Northern Virginia, Confederate States of America, (less Jones' and Robertson's brigades), is hereby detached from the Armageddon Training Corps and will move by first available air transportation to Cloud #3039446, which has been positioned at Rowser's Ford, Virginia. Movement of all troops and horses will be completed no later than dawn on 28 June, 1963.

2. Purpose of this exercise is to re-enact the march of the above-named unit from Rowser's Ford to

the environs of Gettysburg (June 28–July 2, 1863). It is hoped that this re-enactment will demonstrate what the Civil War was really like. For some little time certain quasi-public commissions, patriotic organizations, authors, and other self-styled authorities have been engaging in discussions, mock battles, and other rites, which have tended to deviate a considerable distance from the actual truth. It is expected that this exercise will put an end to the bugling and that people will be able to get back to work on more important things.

3. It is patently impossible to lend the Union Army, in part or in whole, for this exercise. Consequently, opposition will be furnished by such organizations as are readily available to the Supreme Command.

4. Because of the present heavy workload borne by the Department of Miracles and other civil agencies of the Eternal Government, it has been deemed advisable to place certain restrictions on the actions of the Commanding General and all personnel of the Cavalry of the Army of Northern Virginia. They are as follows:

a. No human being is to be killed.

b. Although normal foraging will be permitted, no private home or building is to be destroyed. Such public or semi-public structures as bridges, railroads, etc. may be considered as legitimate military objectives.

c. The members of the command will operate as horse cavalry at all times in order to preserve the spirit of the exercise. They will *only* make use of modern powered transportation when such use is necessary to completion of the mission.

5. The Commanding General will operate at all times under the orders issued to him in June, 1863, by General Lee, *and with such knowledge of the situation as he then had.*

6. Operation will be concluded by 0800 hours of 2 July, 1963, and the command will report to Hill #16069242 for transportation to permanent station.

7. Upon termination of exercise, Commanding General will submit a full report to the Supreme Commander.

By Order of the Supreme Commander
signed/Michael, Archangel, 1st Class,
Chief of Staff

1

☆

Out of the morning mists that hung thickly over the Potomac River a long column of horsemen filed up the riverbank and onto the Poolesville Road. Their dress was nondescript, mostly a vague dust color. Their faces were dirty, unshaved, and streaked with sweat and weariness. For the most part they slumped on their horses, but from time to time one of them would straighten up and look around at his surroundings.

At six-thirty that morning, Mrs. Tom Granville lifted the baby from his high chair and put him in his play pen. After that she dumped a small glass of soap into the automatic washer and turned the switch. The front screen door slammed and her son

Sandy came bounding through the living room to slide to a stop on the kitchen linoleum.

"Mommy," he yelled, "come see the parade!"

"Parade? You must be mistaken, Sandy. There's no parade out here in the country."

"Oh yes, there is. Come and see, Mommy."

Mrs. Granville pulled her housecoat tighter, patted her hair, and made her way out onto the small front porch. A horseman jerked up from his reverie as she appeared, then swept off his hat in a low bow from the saddle. Mrs. Granville looked up and down the road at the long column, then turned and reached into the house to get a small American flag that stood near the door. She handed it to Sandy.

"Just wave this at the men," she told her son. "That's the way to watch a parade."

Having thus provided for the preoccupation of her offspring, she went back into the house, picked up the telephone, and dialed a number.

"Hello, Sally," she said. "This is Gloria Granville. Tell your kids to get out in the front yard. There's some kind of a parade going by."

"They've already discovered it," Sally said. "They're positively wild. I'm making some lemonade for them to sell."

"What kind of a parade is it?" Gloria asked. "Some kind of a circus?"

"No. Ed says he thinks it is some kind of a re-enactment of the Battle of Gettysburg. Next week is the hundredth anniversary."

"Well, thank God for it, anyway. If Sandy just stays out there in the front yard waving that flag, maybe I'll be able to get something done around here."

2

☆

June, 1863
. . . you can move . . . into Maryland and take
position on General Ewell's right, place yourself in communication with him, guard his
flank, keep him informed of the enemy's move-
ments, and collect all the supplies you can.

R. E. Lee to J. E. B. Stuart

General Stuart took off his long gloves and re-
moved the watch from his blouse, then waved his
hand at Brigadier General Fitzhugh Lee.

"Fitz," he said, "it's nine o'clock. I'll leave this
place in your hands. Wade Hampton must be almost to Rockville by now."

"No trouble up ahead. One of my men tells me
the people act right friendly. They seem to think
we're part of some kind of a centennial pageant.
Don't understand it, but if it keeps them friendly,
I say it's good."

General Stuart frowned and rubbed his red
beard.

"Centennial? I can't think what it's the centennial of unless it's the French Indian War." He shook his head, then grinned and winked. "But, if they're happy, it's good." He put his hand up to his big plumed hat and swung around to face the calm, heavily mustached young man beside him. "Coming, Blackford?"

"Yes, sir," Blackford said, and nudged his horse.

The two men cantered up the road out of the heavy morning mist. There were two long columns of riders, one on either shoulder of the highway, but none of the cavalrymen paid much attention to the general and his companion. They were tired and dirty and most of them were still wet from the soaking they had endured while fording the river. If they could, they dozed in their saddles. Those that were awake simply gazed idly at the fresh green countryside as their horses moved along at a slow walk.

There were twenty people lounging in front of a store in Poolesville when the general rode by. When the idlers saw the plumed hat, the ferocious red beard, and the bright yellow sash, some of them clapped. One of them even let loose a mild version of a Rebel yell. The general raised his hat high above his head in a flourish and half bowed from the saddle, but kept on riding.

About half a mile beyond the town there was a white house with a woman and a small child standing on the lawn. The child was waving an American flag. A few yards beyond the house the general stopped.

"Blackford," he said, "be so kind as to order a picket placed below that house. I don't want any misguided patriot taking that flag away from that youngster. You know what John Greenleaf Whittier did to us in Frederickstown." He winked. "Besides, that's a mighty fine-looking woman."

Blackford caught up with the general again another half mile up the highway. The general had stopped to consider a sign that had been set up at the side of the road. The sign said, "Lemonade—Two cents a glass." Two small children were seated on crates behind a makeshift counter on which stood a pitcher and some glasses.

"Lemonade, by gad!" the general said. "Blackford, let's have some."

They reined their horses through the column on the left-hand side of the road. As they dismounted in the drive, a woman in a housecoat came out to the porch of the house. She sat on the railing and held a cup of coffee in her hand. The general looked up, saw her, and strode rapidly across the lawn to stand below her. He swept off his hat with a flourish and bowed low.

"My compliments, madam," he said. "May I present myself? I am General James E. B. Stuart, Confederate States of America. I hope you do not mind if my adjutant and I purchase some lemonade from your children."

The woman smiled and held out her hand.

"Glad to know you, General," she said. "I don't mind in the least. I think they were getting a little discouraged." She signaled the little boy and he ran to the porch with a glass of lemonade. "Billy," the woman said, "meet General Stuart."

"Are you a real general?" the boy asked.

"I am, sir."

"Like General Eisenhower?"

"Never heard of him," General Stuart said.

"You must be a Democrat," the woman said, laughing. "Come up and sit awhile, General."

"Nothing would give me greater pleasure," the general said, shaking his head sadly, "but I'm a soldier and I'm in a hurry." He gulped down the lemonade and smacked his lips. "Magnificent," he said. "Do we pay the children?"

The woman nodded and the general walked to the stand. Taking his wallet from his blouse, he extracted a dollar bill, handed it to the boy, and remounted. He was in the act of waving his hat at the woman when the boy let out a howl.

"Hey! This ain't no dollar bill. This is phony."

The woman came down off the porch and took the money, turning it over and over in her hand.

"You cheapskate," she said. "This is a Confederate dollar bill. Is that any way to treat children?"

"Blackford," the general said, his eyes opened wide in surprise, "have you got any Yankee money?"

Blackford pulled out his purse and fumbled in it, finally pulling out two coins. He threw these to the boy, turned his horse, and followed the general onto the road.

"Hey!" the boy said, looking at the coins, "these ain't no good, either."

"What did you give him?" the general asked, frowning.

"I gave him two two-cent pieces."

The general wheeled his horse. His beard bristled.

"Madam," he said, "enough is enough. We have paid the sum of one dollar and four cents for two glasses of lemonade. You will get no more."

He turned his horse and cantered away, glowering. He continued to glower for several minutes. As he entered Rockville, he and Blackford passed several people standing on the curb. They waved to him and he relaxed a little. By the time he passed the second group he had begun to smile. After waving his hat at the third group he was grinning. At that point, just as he was about to stop and greet some of his admirers, the column stopped.

"Now what?" he exploded. He waved to Blackford to follow and spurred his horse to a gallop.

Within a moment or two he reached a scene of confusion. Two different columns seemed to come together at a street intersection. The general spied a captain who was riding up and down, trying to get things straightened out.

"What's the trouble here?" he asked. "You're holding up the whole advance."

"This is a right confusin' town, General," the captain said. "We got into it all right, but we don't seem to be able to get out of it. There's a road out of here aheadin' for Washington City, and there's a road out of here to Frederickstown, but there don't appear to be no road out of here aheadin' for Pennsylvania. Leastways, we ain't found it. So far, we just went in a complete circle and come right back where we was twenty minutes ago."

The general looked around and then pointed at an old man sitting on the county courthouse steps.

"Blackford, go over there and ask that old fellow how to get to Pennsylvania from here."

Blackford spurred his horse over to the old man.

"You can go to Frederick and take Route 15, or you can go over to Olney and take 97," the old man said.

"We don't want to go to Frederickstown," Blackford said. "Just where is this Olney from here? How do—?"

There was a shout from the corner of the courthouse. Blackford turned to look and saw a man waving his arms wildly and advancing on him.

"Who is he?" Blackford asked the old man.

"He's a cop and you're in trouble. If I was you, I'd move that horse off the lawn before you get run in."

"What's a cop?" Blackford asked.

"You'll find out, soon enough," the man said.

Blackford turned and looked again. The other man was almost up to him.

"Get that horse off the grass," the cop said, and reached for the bridle. The horse reared.

Blackford quieted the animal and looked down at his assailant in an icy manner.

"I wouldn't reach for that bridle again," he said.

The man put out his arm and Blackford quickly drew his saber. The man backed away and stood looking for a moment. Then he made a quick move for the pistol in his holster. Before he got his hands on it two arms reached out from behind and encircled him, then disarmed him. Blackford calmly put the saber back and nodded at the bearded man on the ground.

"Thank you, soldier," he said.

" 'Twarn't nothin'," the soldier said. "I reckoned he was fixin' to get a little ornery so I just sidled over here. What do you want me to do with the critter?"

"He's armed and he's wearing some kind of a

uniform. I reckon that makes him a Yank. Take him prisoner. If you see any more like him, be careful of them."

"Sure be glad to catch me a few Yanks," the soldier said, prodding his captive. "March!"

Blackford turned back to the old man.

"Now," he said, "which way is Olney?"

The old man got to his feet and pointed out the directions. Blackford thanked him and cantered back to where the general was talking to several ladies who were standing on the curb with Confederate flags in their hands.

"Oh, Blackford," the general said, "these ladies tell me they have an organization called the Daughters of the Confederacy here." Blackford took off his hat and bowed to the ladies. The general continued. "Ladies, this is my adjutant, Captain Blackford. If you'll pardon us for a moment, we have a little business to get out of the way." He wheeled his horse and rode off a little distance. After the captain had pointed out the way to Olney, the general nodded. "Very good," he said. "I'll get this column started. You go back there and find out what those ladies want. Make my apologies."

Blackford rode back to the curb where the ladies still stood, clutching their flags in their hands.

"Ladies," he said, "I'm very sorry, but you must understand that the general is a very busy man. He asked me to make his apologies."

"Damn it!" one of the ladies said, causing Blackford to raise his eyebrows. "We wanted him to come and see our clubhouse. It's very nice, you know. If we'd known you people were coming we'd have arranged a reception. Why don't they tell people when they plan something like this?"

"I don't suppose anyone in Richmond knew there was an active group of sympathizers here in Maryland."

"Ladies, how many chapters do we have in Maryland?"

One of the ladies began to count on her fingers.

"Never mind," Blackford said, "it might be best if I didn't know. Perhaps we'll see you another time."

"You couldn't convince the general to just come and sit on our porch and have a cup of coffee with us? It's very pleasant and we'd like to be of service."

"I'm afraid not. Thank you so much, anyway. And now, ladies, if you'll pardon me." Blackford put on his hat and prepared to turn his horse.

"Oh, Captain," one of the ladies said, simpering, "before you go I wonder if you could tell us something?"

"Of course, madam."

"Who's playing the part of General Stuart? I told these ladies that I'd bet it was Maurice Evans. They wouldn't dare let any second-rate actor portray him."

"I don't understand." Blackford looked puzzled.

"You know. In this pageant."

"Ladies, this is no pageant, as the Yanks will soon discover." Blackford lifted his hat and turned away. When he reached a corner of the street he turned and looked back and rubbed the stubble on his chin, then shook his head. He found the general in the middle of a bridge talking excitedly with General Hampton. They were looking over the railing in a perplexed manner.

"I don't know what to make of it," Wade Hampton said. "It's a railroad, right enough, but it's not on any of our maps."

"Looks to me like it runs from Washington City up to Frederickstown," General Stuart said. "In that case, Joe Hooker could use it to bring up supplies and reinforcements." He turned away and paced rapidly up and down for a moment. When he stopped he pointed a finger at Wade Hampton. "Wade, we're going to stop right here and tear it up. How much time will you need?"

"Three-four hours."

The general banged one gloved fist into the other.

"Let's get at it," he said. "Use half your men. Break it up in several places. Use the other half of your command to form small raiding parties of ten or twenty men. Send them down the road toward Washington City and tell them to raise as much hell as they can." His eyes brightened and he grinned widely. "We'll pull old Abe Lincoln's beard a bit." He looked around hurriedly. "I'll have Chambliss take over the advance. Better wind this all up and be ready to move on by four-thirty. If I can find one, I'll set up a headquarters in Rockville. You can find me there."

Blackford stepped forward.

"General," he said, "those ladies offered you the use of their clubhouse. It might be worth looking into."

"Daughters of the Confederacy, eh? Hmmph." The general grimaced. "From what I saw of them they ought to call themselves the Grandmothers of the Confederacy."

"They weren't spring chickens," Blackford said, grinning, "but there were two or three that were passable."

"Well, they'll have to do." The general shook his head. "I just like good scenery. You'll know where to find me if you need me, Wade."

General Stuart and Blackford remounted and cantered back into town. As they reached the courthouse they saw a cavalryman with three men trussed together.

"These are three Yanks, General, just like the one I caught who was tryin' to shoot the cap'n," the soldier said. "I had that other feller all tied up and I was bringin' him out here to the street to wait

for a pack mule when these three came walkin'
aroun' the corner of that buildin' yonder. They see
me with the first feller and they come arunnin'.
They liked to pull me off my horse, but some boys
from the 3rd Virginny give me a hand. These here
are pretty nasty fellers, I can tell you, and they
ain't to be monkeyed with."

"You did well, soldier," the general said.

"I know where there's a whole nest of these
fellers in back of that courthouse buildin'. If you'd
like me, I'll take some of the boys and go get the
whole passel of them."

"By all means," the general said, "do so." He
looked at his watch. "Blackford, do you suppose
those ladies could scare up a little food for us?"

3

☆

June 28, 1863
The men were beset by scores of pretty girls . . .
in Rockville who waved Confederate flags from
windows. . . . Most of the day was spent in
Rockville.

W. W. Blackford,
The War Years with Jeb Stuart

Blackford patted his freshly shaved face and
twisted the ends of his big mustache in a satisfied
manner. He looked out a window and saw the big
Confederate flag hanging from the porch and the
horses of the five-man messenger detail tied to the
branches of the apple tree. He drew in a big breath
and went into the library to see if the general was
still busy writing his letters. There had been some
trouble with that as the ladies had insisted that he
use something they called a ballpoint pen, but
once the general had settled down to his work,
things had subsided and Blackford knew enough
to tiptoe about. While the general scribbled at the
desk, the captain inspected the furniture and the
paintings. When he came to a book lying on a table,

he picked it up, idly flipped through the pages, then carried it back to a chair. The further he read into it, the deeper his frown became.

"General," he said finally, looking up, "you ought to look at this book. Tells what we've done so far."

"What's the name of it?" the general asked, continuing to write.

"It's called *Lee's Lieutenants*. It's sort of a history of the war."

"Can't be much good," the general said, scribbling away. "It's too early for a history. It's probably just some amateur who's putting together the dispatches he clips from the newspapers."

Blackford went back to his reading for a few minutes, then looked up again.

"You're right about this book," he said. "It says we captured a hundred and twenty-five wagons and fiddled around with them so long that we were responsible for losing a battle. I don't recall anything like that."

The general looked up.

"Just how could we lose a battle by capturing a hundred and twenty-five wagons? Seems to me that if we captured that many wagons we'd have *won* the battle."

"I haven't read that far yet. I—"

Mrs. Mabel Alliston, the current captain general of the Rockville chapter came rushing into the room.

"Captain," she sputtered, "you're cutting the pages in our special edition of Freeman."

"I had to read the book," Blackford said, surprised. "How can you read a book without cutting the pages?"

"*That* book wasn't meant to be read."

She held out her hand for it and Blackford gave it to her meekly. Before he had a chance to say anything, there was a loud commotion outside. He walked to the window just in time to see two horsemen come galloping around a corner of the house next door. They rode right across the clubhouse lawn and threw themselves off their horses at the foot of the porch steps. They were unshaved and dirty and their faces were streaked with sweat. Their clothes looked like a series of patches sewn together. Blackford hurriedly stepped through the French doors to intercept them. He stood at the top of the steps and looked down at them.

"Whar at's the general?" one of the men asked.

"What do you want with the general?"

"We got news for the general and we aims to give it to him," the man said.

"What's all this noise?" The general stepped briskly out onto the porch and walked to the steps.

"Howdy, General," the man said. "We got some news about some Federals we run into south of town a piece. Gil Yancey, he's our lieutenant, reckoned we better come over here and tell you about it."

"Who are you men?" the general asked.

"This here's Zeke Carter. Me, I'm Eben Raleigh. We ride with Wade Hampton."

"Just how many Yanks did you scare up, Eben?"

"They ain't but a few Yanks yet, General. What's important is the wagon they was ridin' in. You better come take a look at it."

"What's so unusual about a wagon?"

"They's enough food in this here wagon to feed dang near our whole army."

The general pulled his beard thoughtfully and stole a look at Blackford. Then he seemed to shake himself.

"Eben," he said, "you go back and tell your lieutenant that I don't want to capture any wagons. When we get up to Pennsylvania we'll find plenty of food, anyway."

"What do we do with it?"

"I don't care. Burn it. Anything."

"That don't seem right, nohow," Zeke Carter said. "My cousin Ab, he's up there marchin' with General Ewell and he gets right hungry at times. He could sure use a quarter of beef and I'd be obliged if I could take it to him."

"No," the general said firmly.

"Anything you say, General," Eben said, shaking his head. He and Zeke mounted their horses and rode off dejectedly.

The general watched them go.

"Maybe we ought to go in and take another look

at that book," he said, turning back to the library.

"If I can find it," Blackford said. "That Mrs. Alliston took it away from me."

The general sat down to finish his writing and Blackford began looking around the room for the book. After a few moments there was a sharp knock on the door from the hall and the captain went to see who it was. He found the sergeant of the messenger detail standing awkwardly.

"I'm fearful I got you and the general in some powerful trouble," the sergeant said.

"How did you do that?"

"Some of my squad was looking this place over and one of them went into the kitchen and there was a roast chicken sittin' there on the table, big as life. It weren't much of a chicken, but it were a chicken and this boy was powerful hungry. So he just helped himself. Well, with one thing and another, that chicken jus' didn't last very long. One of them ladies come out in the kitchen and she saw the chicken was gone and she was powerful mad. I mean she was *powerful* mad. She told me we ate up the general's dinner and she didn't want to see hide nor hair of us again."

Blackford shook his head sadly.

"Accidents will happen," he said. "I'll apologize to the ladies. As for the general's dinner, I guess we can find ourselves something to eat."

"Oh, we'll fix that all right. I wouldn't want the

general to go hungry so I just took the liberty of makin' that part right. Just so long as you take care of the ladies."

"You go back out on the porch," Blackford said. "I'll tend to the ladies."

Blackford went back into the library and resumed his search for the book.

"Blackford," the general said suddenly, "give this letter to a messenger and see that it gets back to the river. Fitz Lee left a courier there." He finished sealing the envelope and handed it to the captain, who stepped out into the hall with it. When he turned to start for the porch he almost fell over two of the ladies who were rolling up the rug. Both women seemed on the verge of crying.

"Just look at this," one of them blurted out, and unrolled the rug. There was a long rip in it. The woman pointed at the spurs on Blackford's boots. "Can't you take those things off in the house?"

"Did I do that?" he asked.

"I don't know who did it."

"I'll try to be more careful." He edged past the women and started along the bare hallway to the front porch.

"Captain!" one of the women screamed, and held her hands to her face. Blackford turned to look behind him. His spurs had left a trail of splinters all down the hall. He fairly jumped out onto the porch.

The sergeant of the messenger detail was sitting in a rocking chair with his feet on the railing. When he heard the door slam and turned around to see Blackford he jumped to his feet. As the captain approached him he looked around helplessly, then leaned forward and squirted a stream of tobacco juice over the railing into the flower bed.

"Is that the way you do things in Georgia?"

The man looked around again.

"There warn't no spittoon," he said sheepishly. "Anybody in their right mind ought to have a spittoon handy."

"Get rid of the tobacco," Blackford said sternly.

The man reached into his mouth and extracted a big wad and threw it over the rail and onto the lawn.

"Now get me a messenger."

"Yes, sir." The sergeant walked across the porch to the screen door and bellowed. "Wilkins," he yelled.

There was an answering call from somewhere in the upstairs section of the house, followed by the sound of boots clumping down the stairs. A burly, heavily mustached young man emerged onto the porch carrying his hat in his hand and tucking his shirttail into his pants.

"You want me, Sergeant?" he asked.

"Take this envelope back to the river and deliver it to the courier you will find there," Blackford said. He sniffed. "Have you been drinking, soldier?"

"Just a little nip or two. 'Tain't nothin' to what I'm used to."

He clumped down off the porch, walked over to a tree, unhitched and mounted his horse, and with a wild yell galloped across the lawn and into the street.

"Sergeant," Blackford said, "I think you'd better get your men under control."

"Freddie! Freddie! You come back here!" a woman's voice called from the doorway. A screen door was pushed open and a feminine head poked out. "Oh, I thought you were Freddie Wilkins." The woman giggled and went back into the house. A moment later there was a loud crash. Blackford and the sergeant jumped to the doorway and looked in. The woman was sitting on the floor with an overturned table, a smashed mirror, and two broken vases lying beside her. She shook her head and pursed her mouth and said, "Oooooooh." The door at the other end of the hall opened and three ladies streamed through. They rushed to the woman on the floor and tried to help her to her feet.

"I'm sorry," she muttered. "I just missed the hallway, that's all."

One of the other ladies looked at her.

"Charlotte!" she said. "You're drunk."

"So's Freddie Wilkins," Charlotte said.

The three women half supported, half dragged Charlotte to the end of the hall. As they disappeared Charlotte turned and blew Blackford a kiss. After the door had closed behind them, there was a long drawn-out Rebel yell that was choked off just before the end.

Blackford and the segeant turned just in time to see the general storm out onto the porch.

"What in tarnation was all that noise?"

"One of the ladies had an accident, General. She—"

He was interrupted by the sound of hoofbeats from a horse that was being ridden hard. All three men turned to look as a horseman came galloping around the corner and across the yard. As the rider reached the front steps he swung off the horse and came to a salute.

"Well?" the general said, returning the salute.

"Sir," the man said, "I'm Gil Yancey, First Lieutenant, 2nd North Carolina Cavalry. I guess you didn't understand about them wagons we caught."

"I understood very well," the general said.

"General, those wagons carry more food than I ever saw before."

"I don't care how much food they carry. I do not intend to play nursemaid to a bunch of wagons. It would add days to our journey and the food would all spoil before we ever got it to General Lee."

"That's what you don't understand, General. The food is frozen solid and can't spoil. Besides that, the wagons can go sixty miles in one hour."

The general smiled like an indulgent father.

"Nonsense," he said, "the only thing that can go sixty miles in one hour is a train of cars. I'm afraid—"

A door slammed and the men turned to see Mrs. Mabel Alliston. Her fists were clenched, her eyes flashing.

"Get that horse off the lawn!" she shouted.

The general's eyes widened. He looked at Mrs. Alliston and motioned to Yancey to move the horse.

"All the way off the lawn!" Mrs. Alliston said, advancing, her voice shrill. "And move those other horses, too. Look at the mess they've made of our clubhouse grounds. It's taken us fifty years to create something beautiful and you with your tobacco juice and your horse manure and your spurs have almost ruined it in one morning. You ought to—"

Someone inside the house screamed at the top of her voice. A moment later the screen door slammed open.

"Mabel! Mabel!" A woman burst into view holding her head in her hands.

"What on earth is the matter with you, Helen?" Mrs. Alliston started toward her.

"The back yard!" Helen moaned. "Wait till you see what they're doing in the back yard."

"What are they doing in the back yard?"

"They're killing chickens. They—they cut their heads off and the poor things flop all over the place. It's too awful." Helen collapsed in a heap on the porch. Mrs. Alliston turned, tight-lipped, to face the general.

"General," she said, "I'm afraid I shall have to ask you to leave these premises."

The general's face reddened and he opened his mouth to say something, then thought better of it. Instead, he made what might best be described as a stiff bow.

"Blackford," he said in a tight voice, "maybe we'd better go have a look at Lieutenant Yancey's wagons."

By the time the general and Blackford had retrieved their hats and gloves from the library several more of the ladies had crowded onto the porch. One of these came over to stand at the head of the steps as the two men descended.

"You're not leaving?" the woman asked.

"I have *suggested* that they leave," Mabel Alliston said from her position beside the still-fallen Helen.

"But you can't do that, Mabel," the woman wailed. "They're Confederates."

"I hope I never hear of another Confederate again as long as I live," Mrs. Alliston said.

4

***

☆

June 28, 1863

. . . 125 wagons . . . Such a train we had never seen before . . . bread, crackers, bacon, sugar, hams.

Colonel R. L. T. Beale—9th Va. Cav.

The general, Blackford, and Yancey rode down a grassy slope to the concrete strips of the expressway. The general reined his horse and looked around. A group of people huddled in the parkway, guarded by a ring of horsemen.

"Who are all these people?" the general asked.

"They're Yankees. That one group with all the women and children in it came driving along in their private carriages. The other group was riding in the supply wagons."

"Just what do you aim to do with them?"

"I don't rightly know what to do with them. I reckon it's sort of like having a polecat by the tail."

"They ought to be paroled." The general turned to Blackford. "Blackford, while I look into the matter of these wagons, you see to getting these people paroled." He turned back to Yancey. "How do you know these wagons belong to the Federal government?"

Yancey pointed at one of the trucks.

"What's that say on the side of it, General?"

"It says 'Grand Union' on it."

"I'd say that makes it a Federal wagon, but just come over here and talk to the drivers. You'll see."

Yancey pointed to a man sitting on the ground.

"He seems to be the leader here." He motioned for the man to get to his feet. "What's your name, mister?"

"Wilson Mulcahy," the man said.

"Are you a Union man?"

"I sure as hell am," Mulcahy said.

Yancey looked around the group.

"Are all these men Union men?"

Mulcahy looked around pugnaciously.

"You're damned right. And they're *good* union men."

"All right," the general said, nodding, "bring Mr. Mulcahy over here while I see what's in these wagons."

Yancey led the way to the back of one of the trucks and opened the doors. He reached in and pulled out a package from an open packing box.

"This here's beans," he said. "According to the reading there's enough in this package to feed four people. If that's true, General, there's enough beans right here in this wagon to feed my whole regiment for a year."

The general took the package, hefted it, and turned it over and over to look at it. Then he put it back in the truck and pointed at another box.

"What's in those boxes marked 'TV Dinners'?"

"Danged if I know, General."

"Tell you what we'll do, Yancey. I missed my lunch. You cook up a little of this food and we'll try it out." He turned to Mulcahy. "I'm given to understand that these wagons can go sixty miles in one hour. Is that so?"

"It depends on the traffic," Mulcahy said.

"I don't believe it, but I'll give you a chance to prove it," the general said.

"You mean you'll let me go sixty miles to see if I can do it in one hour?" Mulcahy beamed.

"You show me how fast it will go. I don't know about the sixty miles." The general smiled knowingly.

"I can't even get it into high gear in less than sixty miles," Mulcahy said, disappointed.

The general turned to Yancey.

"After you've tended to getting that food cooked, please make the necessary arrangements for a demonstration of this wagon. I think a guard or two will do. Where are those two men you sent to see me a while back?"

"Eben and Zeke? Zeke's up the road catchin' wagons. Eben's out yonder in that thar tree watchin' for Yankees."

"I'll send someone over to get him."

The general found Blackford in the midst of the second group of prisoners. Blackford looked puzzled.

"Trouble?" the general asked him.

"Only one person agreed to sign a paper that he wouldn't bear arms for the United States. The rest of them called me a Communist. They won't sign. What's a Communist?"

"The Communist movement was connected with the French Revolution of 1848. It had something to do with the workers. I don't see what it has to do with us. Well, if these people expect to be paroled, they'll have to sign the paper. Leave them alone for a while to think about it. They'll change their minds." The general pointed at a tree on a hillside at the edge of the right of way some distance off. "That Eben fellow who came to see us in Rockville is up in that tree. Go bring him here. I have a job for him."

Blackford walked briskly up the hill and along the top of it to the tree. As he reached it he heard a hissing noise and looked up.

"Don't ask no questions," Eben whispered. "Get up here quick."

A hand was thrust down out of the lower

branches and Blackford quickly scrambled up into the foliage. Eben pointed. A quarter of a mile away a figure could be seen climbing the embankment to the edge of the right of way.

"Feller's a Yank," Eben said.

The man came straight to the tree and stopped beneath it. He looked around and picked out a spot with deep grass and stretched out full length on his stomach. Taking a pair of binoculars from a case, he trained them on the scene where the trucks had been pulled off the road. Eben Raleigh poked his carbine down out of the tree until it was aimed right at the man's head.

"Young feller," Eben said quietly, "you jus' get up on your feet with your hands in the air."

The man rolled over on his back and looked up at the carbine.

"Who are you?" he asked.

"Never you mind who I be. Who be you?"

"I'm a state trooper," the man said.

"Reckoned some of you Yanks would come asnoopin' aroun' here. You just lay that pistol on the grass and don' try no funny business."

The man sighed and did as he was told. Eben and Blackford quickly climbed down out of the tree and picked up the gun and binoculars.

"What do you want of me?" the trooper asked.

"Why, I wants you to march, young feller," Eben said. "I wants you to march right over there where the people is. Gil Yancey will be awantin' to talk to you I reckon." He prodded the prisoner with his gun.

When Blackford returned to the group he found the general squatted near a campfire, eating.

"Blackford," the general said, "you better try some of this. It's right good. Don't know how the Yanks thought it up, but I give them credit." He got up and stretched. "Mr. Mulcahy," he said, "I think we'll get started."

Twenty minutes later the general took his watch out of his pocket and looked at it.

"Reckon this is about far enough, Mr. Mulcahy," he said. "This wagon will certainly go fast. How far do you calculate we've come?"

Mulcahy looked at the speedometer.

"Seventeen and four-tenths miles," he said.

"Seventeen miles? But we've only been gone for twenty minutes. That's almost a mile a minute."

"I told you this thing would do sixty miles an hour once I got her rolling."

The general grinned appreciatively, then began doing some mental calculations.

"Have you ever been to Pennsylvania?" he asked.

"That's where I just come from."

"How long did it take you?"

"From the state line? About two hours."

"How long would it take from here to Harrisburg?"

"From here? Three hours, maybe four."

"Can all these wagons go this fast?"

"Most of them."

"Then you'll be going to Harrisburg with me."

"Me? Not me! That's kidnaping and I don't intend to be kidnaped. For your information, I don't even intend to go back where we just came from."

"You don't?" The general rubbed his beard.

"Nope. I'm going to turn you over to the first cop I come to. And there's nothing you can do about it."

The barrel of a carbine came poking down from the shelf at the rear of the cab to rest against Mulcahy's head.

"Young feller," Eben Raleigh said, "when the general says 'turn around,' why, you jus' naturally turn around."

"You wouldn't dare pull the trigger," Mulcahy said, a little less confidently. "That'd be murder."

"Guess it would. You've got three seconds before it happens. One—two—"

"You win," Mulcahy said, slowing the truck.

The general found Blackford waiting for him when the truck rolled up at the roadblock.

"I've made up my mind to have me a few of these wagons no matter what that book said," he told the captain. "It takes them only four hours to get to Harrisburg and I intend to be sitting there with a few of them when General Lee gets there.

You're in charge here. Round up as many of them as you can by five o'clock this evening. Bring them north with you. I will be somewhere around the town of Brookeville and you can report to me there at eight-thirty. By the way, how did you come out with the prisoners. Have they agreed to sign the paper yet?"

"I think I have one they will sign."

"A different one? What does it say?"

"That they will not bear arms against the Confederate States of America."

"I don't see any difference between that one and the other one."

"Neither do I, but they seem to think there's a difference."

The general looked at his watch, then mounted his horse.

"We haven't time to argue with them any further. Bring all of them along to Brookeville when you bring the wagons north. By the time you get there, I'll try and have some kind of an administrative headquarters set up to help."

The general clucked at his horse and cantered up the grass slope toward Rockville.

5

☆

It had started out to be a bad day from the very beginning. Lieutenant Rogers had been on duty at the Frederick Barracks of the Maryland State Police for less than fifteen minutes when he received a phone call from the manager of the Montgomery County Airport.

"I thought you'd like to know that Pamela Hunt Carroll and a plane load of guests arrived here at five this morning. I got a bus and sent them over to Manhunt Farms."

Lieutenant Rogers groaned.

"Got any idea who the guests are?"

"I can tell you this much. *Mister* Carroll has three belly dancers and four Scotch bagpipers in *his* crowd. What do you think that means?"

"Headaches. Headaches for the next three days."

The lieutenant went about the routine business of the post, but he stopped from time to time to mull over whether it would be better to send two troopers over to Manhunt Farms to block the driveway, as a preventive measure, or to reinforce the Olney squad and just pick up the drunken drivers as they whizzed about the countryside.

At about quarter of ten in the morning, while he was still in a foul mood, a call came in from the Montgomery County sheriff's office requesting that extra cars and troopers be assigned to the Rockville area to help direct traffic. It seemed that there was some kind of Civil War Centennial parade passing through the county seat and traffic was beginning to tie up in all directions.

"If you knew there was going to be a parade, why didn't you ask for extra men a week ago?"

"We didn't know there was going to be a parade," the deputy said. "Nobody told us."

The lieutenant dispatched three cars to the area. Less than an hour later he received a telephone call from a woman in Gaithersburg. She was considerably agitated and insisted that a gang of men were tearing up the Baltimore and Ohio Railroad. She could see them from her kitchen window. The lieutenant asked her why she hadn't called the sheriff.

"I've been trying to get him," the woman said.

"No one answers the phone."

"I'll check with the railroad at Cumberland," the lieutenant said.

"We have no section crews in that vicinity," the dispatcher said. "As a matter of fact, we've been trying to find out what's wrong. We've got three eastbound freights tied up west of Germantown and two westbound freights backed up east of Kensington. Our telegraph lines appear to be out and we haven't been able to raise any of our station agents by commercial telephone. Let us know what's up."

Trooper Loftin was trying to straighten out the traffic jam on Route 240 when the lieutenant got to him.

"I'll go and check on it and report back," Trooper Loftin said.

That was the last word the lieutenant heard from Loftin. But that, it developed, was the least of his worries. By one o'clock in the afternoon he had received twenty-nine telephone calls from people who reported everything from mashers to armed robbers. In desperation he put in a call to the sheriff's Silver Spring office.

"If you can't get Rockville, how do you expect us to get them?" a deputy asked. "We even called responsible citizens over there to go and see what was the matter."

"What *was* the matter?"

"We still don't know. The last guy just called back and said he couldn't get in. The door was being guarded."

"Guarded by who?"

"A Confederate soldier."

"Are you kidding?"

"That's what the man said. Look, Rogers, I don't know what kind of a crazy business this is, but I haven't got time to help you find out. We got enough trouble over this way and it's getting worse by the minute."

Between one and two o'clock Lieutenant Rogers dispatched four cars to answer calls and never heard from them again. At two o'clock he called on Hagerstown for ten extra cars. While these were coming to his aid he received a call from a bar on the Rockville Pike that it had been invaded and a band of armed men were stealing all the liquor off the shelves. He reached Trooper Ulrich in Glen Echo and told him to make the long run to Garrett Park. Twenty minutes later he received a call from Ulrich.

"Hello, Rogers," Ulrich said, "I'm on Route 70, about five miles south of Rockville. I got a man here who just stopped me on the road. He says he was held prisoner for more than an hour by a group of men just north of here. They let him go when he agreed not to bear arms for the United States. There are about two hundred more people up there who are still being held prisoner because they won't agree to that."

"Did he say what kind of men and how many there are?"

"About twenty. They all got horses."

"Fifty horses in Gaithersburg. Thirty horses in Garrett Park, a hundred in Rockville, and twenty there. There aren't that many horses in Montgomery County. Where the hell did they all come from and what are they doing?"

"I don't know. This guy thinks they're Communists. Maybe it's the revolution."

"Listen, Ulrich, I've got to have some accurate information. It sounds to me like somebody is hysterical or just plain nuts. Can you sneak up the road and make some kind of an accurate count of just how many horses there are and find out just who these people are? Then I'll know exactly what to do about it."

"I'll do my best, Lieutenant. I'll call you back."

Trooper Ulrich was cautious. He stopped his car a good half mile away from the roadblock, made his way on foot up the grassy slopes of the right of way, climbed a fence, and walked to a tree that overlooked the scene. There he flopped down in the grass and put his binoculars up to his eyes. Nothing more was heard from Trooper Ulrich.

A half hour later, while he was still waiting hopefully for a radio call from Ulrich, Lieutenant

Rogers received a phone call from the commander of the Laurel district.

"You having trouble with guys on horseback over your way?" Laurel asked him.

"My district is full of guys on horseback," Rogers said. "You got some, too?"

"I've had seventy-one calls since one o'clock. They're stealing chickens, pigs, cows, horses, booze —anything that isn't tied down. They're cleaning out the county."

"What are you doing about it?" Rogers asked.

"I've been chasing them."

"Caught any of them yet?"

"Not yet, but I expect to. I got all my cars out on the job. You caught any of them?"

"No. I can't even find out who they are."

"Oh, I know who they are," Laurel said. "They're crazy kids. Some of them are carrying Confederate flags."

"I got news for you. Most of those crazy kids have got beards. Look, we got to do something. How many of these guys have been reported in your district so far?"

"About eighty. They all seem to be on Route 97."

"Eighty? My God! If yours are different than mine, then there must be almost three hundred of these crazy bastards loose between you and me. Now, I know we got to do something and we got to do it quick. Get your map out and tell me where your calls have come from."

"The first call came at two minutes after one from Norbeck Corner. Since then I've had calls from the Brooke Manor Country Club, Martin's Dairy, Moore's Egg Farm, Olney—Say! These guys are headed straight up Route 97."

"That's the way it looks to me. Now, look here. If we put a roadblock at the fork of the road there, just south of Roxbury Mills, they'd run right into it."

"That's right."

"The thing is, we got to get enough men to do the job. We're dealing with three hundred armed men on horses. How long do you figure before they get to Roxbury Mills?"

"At the rate they're going, the first ones ought to be there between five and five-thirty."

Rogers looked at his watch.

"I've got ten men here from Hagerstown," he said. "I'll leave here in five minutes and I'll use Route 40 so I'll be there in plenty of time. Call the Baltimore and Howard County sheriffs and the Westminster and Baltimore barracks. Get as many men as you can, even if they have to deputize people. The main thing is to get them moving and get them moving quick. Then call Annapolis and tell them what we're up against. There's a good chance we might even need a company of National Guardsmen. You got everything straight?"

"Will do." There was a pause from the other end of the phone. "Just for the hell of it, Rogers, who do *you* think we're up against?"

"The Confederate Army. Who else?" Rogers laughed and hung up.

6

☆

June 28, 1863

Stuart had some 400 prisoners and paroled them with meticulous regard for the code of war. Officers . . . spent ten or twelve hours working on [the parole papers] in the villages of Brookeville and Cooksville.

Burke Davis, *Jeb Stuart, The Last Cavalier*

At six o'clock General Stuart reached the headquarters Colonel Chambliss had established in a potato field.

"After Fitz Lee passed us, I ordered a halt," the colonel said. "We're strung out along here for five or six miles. The food is good. We have us a mighty fine pig and we'd be honored if you'd eat with us."

"I appreciate your hospitality, but I think I'd better find a house I can use as a headquarters."

"You might try up the road a half mile. My men tell me there is a fine big plantation house up there."

"I'll look. Any messages from Fitz Lee?"

"Yes, sir. He ran into some Yankees up ahead. They have a roadblock at a place called Roxbury

Mills. The force guarding it doesn't appear to be large. Fitz thinks they are trying to delay us until they can get up reinforcements. He wants permission to drive them out of there."

The general paced up and down.

"That'll be locals," he said. "Judson Kilpatrick won't be far behind." He smacked one glove into the other. "I'll be hanged if I'll stand still until he gets ready to fight. We'll just let Judson have his roadblock. Colonel, I hate to spoil your supper, but I want you to take a regiment and go up there. You relieve Fitz. Send in about twenty men at a time, as though you were building up strength to attack. You can play-act all you want to, but every time you put twenty men on the line be sure Fitz pulls out forty. One of our objectives is to tear up the main line of the railroad at Sykesville and I want no delay in that. You tell Fitz, after he's relieved, to find another road to Sykesville and to get up there as fast as he can. And, Colonel, if you like, you can take along a battery of artillery with you to keep the Yanks interested." He grinned. "Put on a good show, but don't get in any fight. Along about three in the morning, pull out and ride after us. By the time old Judson Kilpatrick is ready to fight, we'll be long gone." He looked around. "Now, where's this house you told me about?"

"I'll send an officer to show you," the colonel said. "It's a place called Manhunt Farm."

Manhunt Farm was the ancestral home of Pamela Hunt Carroll. Pamela was a famous horsewoman and an equally famous collector of husbands. In the summer of 1963 she was busy taming her fifth husband and preparing her fifteenth crop of thoroughbreds to race in the Butterscotch and Old Fuchsia silks. After a coupon-clipping expedition to New York, she had plucked her husband from an obscure bar on the East Side and had brought him and his friends of the moment down to Maryland. Her fifth husband was Chris Carroll, a buccaneer at heart. He liked to think of himself as romantic, swashbuckling, and a man of many sides. He was a little hard to live with, too, and Pamela had long ago discovered that it was unwise to interrupt whatever project he might be embarked on at the moment. As a consequence, she had adopted the policy of transporting him and his entourage down to Manhunt Farm where she could wean the hangers-on with good hard liquor. She had perfected what might be called a standard operating procedure of giving her guests just long enough to sleep themselves into a beautiful hangover, then awakening them to start a house party to which anyone could invite such guests as he chose. By the time the party was over, most of her husband's guests would have disappeared, never to be seen again. Pamela didn't have them murdered. She just loaded them on a bus and took them to the airport, where her private plane flew them off to Bermuda or some other place from which it was hard to return.

Pamela had begun things at two in the afternoon. She had roused everyone from bed, had them herded into the grand ballroom, and had then descended the staircase to clap her hands and wave her cigarette holder in the air.

"We're going to have a party," she announced.

As though on signal, a portable bar rolled into the center of the room. As Pamela retired up the stairs to get dressed, Chris Carroll rubbed his hand across his forehead and made his way to the bar. After four quick shots of straight gin, he began to feel better and looked around. He discovered one of the bagpipers standing near the door and re-called that he had been in the midst of proving a new theory of his. Somewhere, sometime in the pre-ceding week, it had struck him that the ideal instru-ment for accompanying a belly dancer was a Scotch bagpipe. He clapped his hands.

"Pipers, let's get started," he said, and leaned back against the bar to sip his first martini of the day.

It was at some point during these opening cere-monies, while the belly dancers were still warming up and while most of the other guests were scurry-ing around to find telephones to invite other guests, that the first horsemen appeared. In a place as con-fused as Manhunt Farm usually was it would be difficult to determine just when they made their presence known. Ten of them had galloped up the long gravel drive from the main highway. Five had gone to the house. The other five had debouched upon the outer acres. Eventually the latter group had discovered more than sixty absolutely perfect cavalry mounts and had lost no time in rounding them up and driving them off toward the highway. The five men who had gone to the house had come to stand in the open doorway of the ballroom and watch the belly dancers with eyes popping. Chris Carroll saw them and went to greet them. *He* thought they were guests, naturally. It was no chore at all for him to be pleasant to five men who introduced themselves as members of the 7th Virginia Cavalry. When they announced that they had come to inspect the premises, Chris Carroll took them off on a personally escorted tour. Somewhere between the master bedroom and the maid's smoking room, Chris was struck with the authenticity of their speech and manners. He stopped and addressed them.

"By God!" he said. "I don't know why I didn't think of it before. We need something different in the way of a party around here. We'll have a Civil War Centennial party and no one can come but Confederates." He patted his guests on the back affectionately. "You fellows make yourselves at home while I go and get things started."

He bounced joyfully down the grand staircase, put his fingers to his mouth and whistled, then made his announcement. While everyone scurried off to fulfill the new edict as best he could, Chris marched across the ballroom to the four bagpipers and instructed them to start playing "Dixie" and to play until he told them otherwise. Having thus set the mood for the party, he bounded back up the staircase to start digging in the trunks for the uniform he had worn to the première of *Gone With the Wind*.

While Chris Carroll was on the second floor, robing, the manager of Manhunt Farm came skidding up to the big house in his jeep and rushed through the library doors to confront Pamela. He announced that some villains were driving off sixty head of her best blooded stock. She jumped into the jeep and was driven to the main gate, where she faced the five horsemen. She got nowhere. She had to stand and watch, helpless, while the horses were driven off.

Pamela Hunt Carroll may have taken a cavalier attitude toward husbands, but about horses she was dead serious. When she got back to the big house she marched into the library, closed all the doors, and got busy on the telephone. She started at the local government level and worked gradually up to the Federal government.

While Pamela was still busy on the telephone,

her husband made his grand entrance down the staircase clad in the uniform of a Confederate cavalry captain. Shortly after he reached the ballroom he remembered his five special guests from the 7th Virginia. He finally discovered them in the kitchen busily devouring a ham set out for them by a hospitable cook who was trying to pump them for the latest news from his home town in the Blue Ridge. With one of them still hanging onto the ham bone, Chris escorted the soldiers into the ballroom and there promptly introduced them to the martini and explained the intricacies of belly dancing, now being done quite successfully to the strains of "Dixie."

General Stuart arrived on the scene as the five members of the 7th Virginia Cavalry were gulping down their third drink. He mounted the steps at one end of the huge front porch and progressed toward the front door. Just before he reached the entrance he passed an open window and the five soldiers saw him. Without a word they streaked through the house, ducked onto the veranda at the far end, and disappeared around a corner. A moment later Chris Carroll, martini in hand, came to the front door to stick his head out to see where his guests had gone. He stopped and stared.

"Magnificent," he said. "Absolutely superb."

"Captain," the general said, his eyes wide, "would you be kind enough to explain yourself?"

"I was referring to the beard," Chris Carroll said. "I haven't seen anything like it outside of the pictures of old Jeb Stuart."

"Sir," the general said, "I am old Jeb Stuart."

Chris Carroll looked at the general, then cast a suspicious glance at his martini. He shuddered, took hold of himself, and came to attention as stiffly as he could. Transferring his drink to his left hand, he saluted with his right.

"I am honored," he said.

The general looked him over from head to foot.

"Captain," he said grimly, "I rather expect my men to get drunk from time to time. I expect my officers to hold *their* liquor. To what unit do you belong, sir?"

"Unit?" Chris Carroll was only momentarily confused. Then he brightened. "I am not at present assigned to any unit, sir. I guess you would say I'm on recruiting duty."

"In Maryland?" the general scowled.

"I own this place. Or rather my wife does." He stood to one side and extended his arm toward the door. "Please accept the hospitality of this house."

The general hesitated, looked again at Chris, then strode forward. As he passed into the ballroom, Chris signaled to the bagpipers for a fanfare, then held up his hands.

"Ladies and gentlemen," he announced in his best voice, "I have the very great honor to present

Lieutenant General J. E. B. Stuart, Confederate States of America."

Five minutes later, after the general had become stalled halfway down the reception line by the three belly dancers, Chris let himself into the library where Pamela had got up to the Assistant Secretary of the Navy.

"Come out and meet General Stuart," Chris said.

"I don't want to meet any of your damned characters," Pamela said. "Don't you realize that somebody has stolen sixty head of my best stock?"

"I think I may have the man who is responsible for it," Chris said.

"If you've got him, go out and shoot him. Do something, just once in your life, to justify your existence."

There was a squawk from the other end of the phone. Pamela looked at it and put it up to her ear.

"—and I don't see why you called *me*, Pamela," a voice said. "The loss of sixty horses is not a Navy matter. As far as the Confederate Army is concerned, the only people I know who would have any jurisdiction would be the Civil War Centennial Commission. Why don't you call them?"

"Oh, the hell with you!" Pamela banged the phone into its cradle.

"Why don't you try it my way?" Chris asked her.

Pamela glared balefully out at the ballroom.

"It better work," she said, getting to her feet.

"Steady, old gal!" Chris said, following her out the door. "Remember your manners. He's a guest, you know."

A moment later they stood before the general.

"Please allow me, sir. My wife Pamela. Pamela, Lieutenant General J. E. B. Stuart. I don't mind telling you, sir, that Pamela is a little miffed right now. Some of your men have run off sixty head of her best stock."

"Horses?" the general said.

"Thoroughbreds," Pamela said. "The finest racing and breeding stock in the country."

General Stuart turned to the officer who had accompanied him from Colonel Chambliss' headquarters.

"Find out who took those horses, Major. I want them returned immediately. It is not our business to rob ladies, especially those who support us."

"You mean it?" Pamela asked, her mouth open.

"I do."

"General, you're a little bit of all right. Come and meet my other guests." She took him by the arm.

The general was in the midst of a special performance by the belly dancers when Captain Blackford arrived. The captain pointed down at the driveway.

"There's four hundred and seven people in two hundred and sixty-eight carriages in that line," he said.

"What a traffic jam," Chris Carroll said.

"I wouldn't want to take them any further," Blackford said, mopping the perspiration from his forehead. "But we need a place to register their parole papers."

"I have already spoken to Mrs. Carroll. She has been kind enough to grant us the use of her library."

"We have seventeen of those Maryland state troopers. We had to manacle them with their own manacles. I don't think we ought to release them."

"We ought to be able to take seventeen of them along with us. How many wagons did you get?"

"One hundred and twenty-five." Blackford looked down at the toe of his boots.

"One hundred and twenty-five?" The general's smile disappeared. "Did you plan it that way?"

"No, sir. It just happened."

"Well, I don't see how they could hold us up." The general shrugged and resumed his smile.

"General," Blackford said, "I think you ought to know, we've already had trouble with them."

"What kind of trouble?"

"It's got something to do with the Union."

"The Union? Gad, man, we have to expect some trouble with the Union. These Yanks aren't going to lie down and play dead, you know. They never have yet."

"This is a different kind of trouble. The drivers claim to have something called a negotiating committee. They want to talk to you."

"All right, bring them on as soon as we get this mess straightened out." He pointed at the line of cars.

It was Chris Carroll who untangled the traffic jam. He stood on the veranda with a martini in one hand and a cavalry saber in the other and shouted orders to five pairs of Maryland state troopers who stood, handcuffed together, at strategic points. As the last auto nosed into the polo field, Blackford came striding to the porch, accompanied by several cavalrymen and five of the truck drivers.

"This is something that claims to be a negotiating committee," Blackford said when the party had come to stand at the foot of the steps leading to the porch.

"I see Mr. Mulcahy there," the general said. "What have you got to do with this, Mulcahy?"

"I been appointed chairman of this committee," Mulcahy said. "We want some things settled. We don't like the idea of being ordered around like sheep. We don't let the owners do it and we ain't going to let you do it. It ain't democratic and we don't have to take this kind of crap. This is the United States of America, you know."

"I know," the general said, "but I don't think the United States of America is in any position to help you right now. It just so happens that you are my prisoners. As my prisoners you have no choice."

Mulcahy folded his arms and looked up at the general in a pugnacious manner.

"I'll tell you one thing," he said. "I been authorized to tell you that our trucks ain't going to move another foot from where they are. This is a strike."

"We're moving north shortly," General Stuart said calmly, "and those wagons will move with us."

"They won't," Mulcahy said.

The general turned to Blackford.

"You will please take a message to General Hampton," he said. "He is to appoint a provost guard of two hundred men. These wagon drivers will be formed into a column and marched back to Richmond. When they reach Richmond they will be interned at hard labor until I return to conduct their trial. You may say that I insist on the letter of these orders. *These men will walk every foot of the way back to Richmond!*"

"You're not scaring us," Mulcahy said. "We're not moving from this spot. As a matter of fact, we're establishing a picket line." He nodded to one of the men, who pulled out some signs. They read: "Jeb Stuart and the Civil War Centennial Commission is unfair to organized labor."

General Stuart looked at the group and his eyes

finally came to rest on Eben Raleigh. The general winked solemnly and Eben came to something that resembled attention, did an about-face, and marched to the rear of the formation. From there he aimed a kick that caught Mulcahy squarely in the seat of the pants.

"When the general says 'git,' you git."

Mulcahy looked carefully down at his fist, pulled it back, and let it fly. Eben Raleigh sat down on the seat of his pants and looked up at the truck driver.

"Ain't no Yankee goin' to do that to me," he said, scrambling to his feet. He lowered his head and plowed forward like a battering ram, catching Mulcahy in the stomach. In a matter of moments the whole drive was a mass of flying arms and legs. The fight didn't last long because the drivers were badly outnumbered. By the time they were hauled to their feet, all of them were pretty badly bruised.

"Now, damn you, march!" Eben Raleigh said, aiming another kick at the seat of Mulcahy's pants.

Blackford followed down the driveway to where the drivers had lit a huge bonfire in a field across the road from Manhunt Farm. They were gathered in a huge circle around it.

"I resign," Mulcahy said to them.

"You can't do that, Wilson," one of the drivers said. "You're the most experienced guy we got. You're president of a local."

"I ain't going to get beat up again."

"What do they agree to?"

"To let us drive those trucks. And if we don't drive them, we're going to *walk* to Richmond."

"What do you think we ought to do?"

"Drive the trucks."

"But the union can't back down like that."

"Back down or walk. These babies mean business and they got all the cards. I think we ought to vote on it. All those in favor of walking, raise your hands."

No one raised his hand.

"You saw the vote," Mulcahy said to Blackford. "We'll drive, but we want one thing understood."

"What's that?" Blackford asked.

"We want the general to promise to observe our working rules."

"I'll go back and tell the general," Blackford said. "In the meantime, if I were you, I'd get some rest. You'll be moving about midnight."

Blackford mounted his horse and rode back up to Manhunt Farm and reported to the general.

"Good," the general said. "I wish you'd look and see how the paroles are coming. Captain Carroll, here, has asked to have a word with me. I'll be along shortly."

"I'm sorry to bother you, General," Chris Carroll said, after Blackford had gone, "but I've been hoping to get a chance to talk to you."

"Of course, Captain."

"I should like to apply for active service. I want to go north with you. As a veteran of the war in the Pacific I am not exactly a neophyte in military affairs."

"What war in the Pacific?" the general asked.

Chris Carroll opened his mouth twice to say something. Each time he closed it again and shook his head.

"I—I was in Japan," he said weakly.

The general's whole demeanor changed. He took a step back, cocked his head, and looked at Chris Carroll with genuine interest.

"Were you really with Perry?" he asked. "Now, that *is* interesting, Mr. Carroll. That *must* have been an experience and I'd like to hear about it. Of course, I'd hardly call it a war. I think of it as a diplomatic feat."

"Whatever it was, I was there."

The general looked at Chris in admiration.

"Captain Carroll," he said, "let me consult with my commanders. Maybe we can find a place for you with your gifts." He took Chris by the arm. "Come along. Let's go have a look at how the paroles are coming."

The two men walked out to the veranda. Down at one end of it was a long line of people waiting to get into the library. Upon arrival there they found Captain Blackford arguing vehemently with a young man and his wife who were standing before a desk.

"I never heard of any state of Idaho," Blackford said. "You're going to have to tell us the truth if you expect to be released."

"I've told you ten times that we come from Pocatello, Idaho," the man said. "And that's the truth."

Blackford threw up his hands and turned to the general.

"I don't know what to do with these people," he said. "What we need here is an experienced diplomat."

"Diplomat?" General Stuart said. "Did you say diplomat?" He turned and looked at Chris Carroll.

"But I was hoping for combat," Chris Carroll said. "The last time I had to spend the whole war as a PX officer. Now I can't even get into the Civil War."

"Mr. Carroll," the general said, patting him on the back, "you're a good soldier and I'll make you a promise. When you finish this job you ride north and report to me, personally. I'll not only make you a member of my staff but I'll see to it that you get all the action you ever wanted."

Chris Carroll drew himself to attention, switched his martini to his left hand, and saluted.

7

June 28–29, 1863

He hung onto . . . the Federal wagons as if they were the only evidence of his success. The drivers grumbled and the wagons often became tangled in disarray.

Burke Davis, *Jeb Stuart, The Last Cavalier*

At approximately eleven o'clock a horseman had come galloping up to the Carroll mansion with a message.

"No difficulty with Federal troops at Roxbury Mills. Our route leads east around a large lake which does not appear on the maps. Have left guides at junction of Road 97, point where you turn east. Do not waste time exploring roads as I have already explored them at some delay to myself. Most of them only lead into lake. Guides know route. Expect you at Sykesville at dawn. Signed— Fitzhugh Lee."

The general bowed graciously to Pamela Hunt Carroll, kissed her hand, and went out to his horse. As he and Blackford reached the main highway, they found the trucks lined up with their motors running. Far up the road, at the head of the column, Mulcahy and his road committee studied a map by the headlight on Mulcahy's truck.

"You know what to do?" one of the men asked.

"Sure. I been up this road before. If they take the left fork at Roxbury Mills, we take the right. And vice versa. I'll make it all right. Just you guys close up and keep closed up. We've got about a three-mile grade here and when I break over the top of it, I'm going to shove it up to fifty. They'll never be able to catch us on those horses at that speed, but everybody's got to stay together." He looked up to see Blackford approaching and folded the map and put it away, then winked solemnly at his fellow conspirators.

"You will please turn out all the lamps, Mr. Mulcahy," Blackford said.

"But we can't drive without lights."

"We don't need lights on our horses. I don't think you need them on your wagons. This is a military movement and your lights would show the Yanks where we're going."

"No lights, no move," Mulcahy said. "The agreement was that we'd drive these trucks wherever you wanted them to go as long as you'd abide by the rules of the road."

"Mr. Mulcahy," Blackford said calmly, "the agreement was that you'd drive those trucks to keep from marching all the way back to Richmond."

"One of the principles of collective bargaining is that each side gives in a little," Mulcahy said. "We gave in on your demands to drive the trucks. You got to give us something in return."

"What is collective bargaining?" Blackford asked.

"You mean you don't know what collective bargaining is?" Mulcahy scratched his head, then let his hands drop helplessly. "Captain, you got to listen to reason. We got to have lights. If you'd get up there in the cab with me, you'd see quick enough. All I ask is for you to be reasonable."

"All right," Blackford said, "I'm reasonable."

He dismounted and followed Mulcahy to the cab and crawled in. Mulcahy put the truck in gear and moved it forward two hundred yards.

"Remarkable," Blackford said, putting out his hand for Mulcahy to stop. "You are right, but I can't understand why you can't get along without lights when we don't need them at all. Frankly, Mr. Mulcahy, I don't think these new wagons will ever be worth much."

"We can have lights, then?"

"You can have lights. The rest of the wagons can have none. They can follow you."

"Can't they just put their guide lights on?"

"What are they?"

"They're the three little ones at the top of the

trailers. The—er—enemy can't see them."

"All right," Blackford said.

"Now that is collective bargaining," Mulcahy said.

"It's no good," Blackford said. "It wasted thirty minutes. Get the wagons moving."

The trucks began creeping forward. For two miles Blackford cantered alongside Mulcahy's cab, his pistol laid conspicuously in front of him. As the column climbed a hill five horsemen loomed up in the middle of the road. They motioned for Mulcahy to turn into a side road to the right. Mulcahy stopped his truck and climbed down into the road.

"You're going to Sykesville, ain't you?"

"We're going there, yes," Blackford said.

"Then you're taking the wrong road," Mulcahy said. "I been to Sykesville before and that's the road there." He pointed straight ahead.

"Mr. Mulcahy," Blackford said, "it makes no difference to me how we get to Sykesville as long as we get there. Get back in that wagon and get it moving." He waved his pistol menacingly and looked back along the column. "You other drivers get back in your wagons, too."

"You're not going to let him get away with that, are you?" one of the drivers asked Mulcahy. "That spoils everything. We have to get to that fork in the road."

Mulcahy looked at the man, then back at Blackford.

"Listen, you hayseed," he exploded, "I'm representing these men here and I say we can't drive down this road. We could get fined for exceeding load limits."

Blackford looked at his watch and prodded Mulcahy.

"You've got till I count three, Mr. Mulcahy."

Mulcahy shrugged his shoulders and started to climb back in his cab, then turned to the other drivers.

"There'll be other forks in the road," he said.

"Be damned sure you don't miss them," a driver said.

Mulcahy made the turn. He had crawled along the side road for several yards before he realized that Blackford had remained at the corner to see that all the trucks turned. He sat up and grinned to himself. In the long beam of his lights he could see the horsemen. They slouched in their saddles, half of them asleep. Slowly he increased his speed. Within ten minutes he was up to thirty miles an hour. At the end of two miles he saw the fork in the road he had been hoping for. The column of horsemen was taking the right fork. The left fork was empty as far as he could see ahead. He reached down and blinked his lights twice in the signal that he was going to run for it. The truck picked up more speed and the big diesel began to roar. Mulcahy could see the horsemen on either side sit up in their saddles as the noise reached a crescendo. They were too late. With a blast of his air horn, Mulcahy guided the truck through the gap between the tail of one horse and the head of another. The column was behind him. He shifted into high gear. He could see the lights of the other trucks as they flashed on behind him.

Mulcahy had gone three quarters of a mile when there was a change in the road. It began to curve to the left and to drop downhill. Another four hundred yards and the macadam ended abruptly. The truck shot out onto a gravel road. On the right a sign flashed by, but Mulcahy couldn't read it. The sign was followed closely by a fence. After that there was no more gravel—only a deeply rutted road that dropped downward steeply. With some alarm, Mulcahy applied his brakes and within a hundred yards the headlong flight had slowed to a crawl. Then it stopped altogether. The road just ran into a lake and in the headlight beams there was nothing but a wide expanse of water. From behind him Mulcahy heard the sound of an angry voice.

"Come on up here and you'll see why I stopped," he shouted back to the truck behind.

The truck drivers began to gather at his bumper.

"It's the Patuxent Reservoir," one of them said. "I should have remembered it was here."

"Isn't there any other road out of here?" Mulcahy asked, looking around desperately.

"Nope. Just the one the cavalry was taking."

More truck drivers edged forward to look. It was a full ten minutes before the first horseman arrived.

"Well, I declare. A lake." Eben Raleigh edged his horse forward into the fringe of light. "You fellers is about the orneriest fellers I ever seen," he said, then looked around as Blackford came galloping up. "What do you want we should do with them, Cap'n?"

"They can back those wagons out of here."

"You mean you want us to back these trailers up this country road for two miles?" Mulcahy asked.

"That is just what I want," Blackford said.

"We can't. They'd jackknife all over the place."

"Then turn them around."

"Where?" The truck drivers turned to look at the dense woods that surrounded them in the darkness.

"Eben," Blackford said, "you'd better go back and see how many axes you can find. It looks like these wagon drivers are going to have a lot of chopping to do."

8

☆

The first group of fifty horsemen had appeared at the Roxbury Mills roadblock shortly after five o'clock in the afternoon. They had ridden over the rise of a hill in casual fashion, but had stopped almost immediately. For the brief span of two minutes they had remained on the skyline, but Lieutenant Rogers had only thirty men behind the barricades at that time and did not consider this a large enough force with which to do battle. As swiftly as the opportunity had presented itself it disappeared. The horsemen, sensing their danger, had spurred off into the woods on either side. They were never seen clearly again. Rogers immediately got on the radio to Laurel.

"I'm going to leave them alone for a while," he said. "The longer they wait the less chance they'll have because *I'll* soon have three hundred men. I'm going to take a scouting party and see if I can find out who they are and what they think they're doing. Let me know about that unit from the National Guard. I think I'll be needing them."

With two men Rogers moved cautiously to the slope of the hill that faced the spot where the riders had last been seen. There he was brought up short by a voice from his immediate front.

"Hey, Yank, jus' don' come no closer. Hear?"

"We hear you," Rogers said.

"You fellers got any coffee over there?" the voice asked. "We got a little genuine Virginny plug over here and we's ready to do a little business. We got a few other things y'all might like to dicker for, too."

Rogers scratched his head.

"Who are you men?" he shouted.

"Now, looka here, Yank," the voice said, "we didn't go askin' y'all any questions like that, now, did we? All we want is some of that there coffee. It would taste right good. We ain't askin' no questions about who we be tradin' with. We just aim to do a little business."

"Look, you men over there, I don't know who you are or what you think you're doing, but I'll tell you who I am. I'm Lieutenant Rogers of the

Maryland state troopers. I want you to surrender
to me."

This speech was followed by a long silence.

"Shucks, Yank," the voice finally said, "we was
only tryin' to be sociable. Whyn't y'all be sensible?
As for surrenderin', why, we got a answer for that."

As the voice ceased speaking the whole hillside
opposite Rogers erupted with flame as firearms of
all kinds were shot off in one volley.

"And there's lots more where that came from,"
the voice said. "It ain't as good as Virginny plug,
but if it's what y'all want, then it's what y'all's goin'
to get. Next time we-uns is agoin' to shoot a mite
lower."

Lieutenant Rogers arrived back at the roadblock
on his belly and grabbed for the radio.

"I want that Guard outfit," he said. "I can't do
anything without it. I'll wait until it gets here."

For the next four hours Rogers sat and gloomily
contemplated the hill in front of him. At a quarter
of twelve he talked to Annapolis for the fifteenth
time.

"Just calm down, Rogers," Annapolis said. "It
takes time to assemble a National Guard unit. The
guns are coming. What have you been doing in the
meantime?"

"I've been sitting here behind these barricades,
trying to keep from being shot. About every twenty
minutes those fellows over there cut loose with a

volley and each time those bullets get a little closer."

"Anybody been hurt?"

"Not yet, thank God. I've got the whole area south of Route 40 cordoned off and I've ordered all the people who live in the area to stay in their houses. I don't know how long our luck will hold out, though."

"Just do the best you can."

The antitank platoon arrived at three-fifteen in the morning. Rogers was almost frothing at the mouth.

"Where in hell have you guys been?" he asked the young captain in charge.

"We'd have been here two hours ago if we hadn't run into a big traffic jam west of Ellicott City," the captain said. "I finally had to go up and direct traffic myself."

"A traffic jam at this hour of the night?"

"That's what I'd call it. Cars were backed up for three miles or more. There was some kind of a procession crossing the highway at Route 32. No one could get through."

"Procession? What kind of a procession?"

"I think it was a circus or something like that. Anyway, I saw a lot of horses and riders and—"

"Horses?" Lieutenant Rogers swung around and looked at the hill opposite. "Horses?"

"That's right. I—"

There was a loud boom, followed by the rattle of small-arms fire.

"Hit the dirt!" Rogers yelled. The sound of pinging bullets could be heard.

"Gets closer every time," someone said.

Lieutenant Rogers turned around to speak to the captain. The captain wasn't there.

"Ouch!" The captain's voice came from somewhere to the rear. "God damn it! This thing is hot."

"What's hot?" Rogers asked.

"I don't know for sure." There was a momentary flash of light that showed the captain's face. "Well, I'll be God-damned! It's a cannon ball."

"What's a cannon ball?"

"This thing that just came from over there."

"You're kidding," Lieutenant Rogers said.

"If that isn't a cannon ball I never saw one," the captain said, handing it to Rogers.

Rogers juggled the ball in his two hands.

"I've had enough of this," he said. "Bullets and cast-iron cannon balls are no joke. Now I'm going to give them a dose of their own medicine." He turned to the captain. "Get your guns in position and tell me when you're ready to fire."

It was ten minutes of four before Rogers gave his command. The weapons of all three hundred police officers and the antitank guns of the National Guardsmen spewed forth a volley onto the hill south of the roadblock. Then a sound truck rolled into place.

"Now hear this," it blared forth. "You men over there on that hill have seen that we have a few guns, too. And what you've seen is only a demonstration. We'll give you exactly one half hour to surrender peaceably. After that we're going to blast you out of there."

There was only silence from across the valley. At four-thirty the barricade once more spewed forth a murderous barrage. This time it lasted for a full twenty minutes and set fire to the undergrowth, plowed up the earth, and knocked trees into splinters. When it was over, a long line of men came out from behind their shelter and stalked slowly across the low ground to the battered hill. In the dawn they found only a few lukewarm campfires to let them know that someone had actually occupied this ground. Lieutenant Rogers leaned against a tree and cursed.

"Just once," he said, "I'd like to catch one of those guys. Just one man."

One of the sheriff's deputies pulled his sleeve and pointed south down the road toward Olney.

"I think you're going to get your wish."

Five horsemen were riding up the road in the early light toward the hill. They were dressed in the gray uniform of the Confederate Army. And they were singing.

"Those guys are *really* crocked," the deputy said.

The riders came on, blissfully unaware that they were being watched. When they reached the hill, Lieutenant Rogers stepped out from behind a tree, strode rapidly over to the leader, and grabbed the book that he carried.

"Confederate Marching Songs," he read aloud. "Just who the hell do you think you are, anyway?"

"I am Captain Christopher Carroll."

Lieutenant Rogers spat on the ground.

"I should have known what this was," he said. "Just where the hell do you think you're going?"

"To Pennsylvania to fight the Battle of Gettysburg."

"You can fight it from jail. If you're lucky, you'll get out in time to celebrate the second centennial."

"Would you tell me what you intend charging me with?" Chris Carroll asked, with great dignity.

"Drunk and disorderly is good enough to start with. After that I'll book you on suspicion of grand larceny, malicious destruction of property, and a few things I haven't even thought of yet."

"You'll never get away with it," Chris Carroll said solemnly. "I may be drunk, but I'm no more drunk than usual. As for being disorderly, since when is it disorderly to ride a horse on the public highway? I'll have you know this road was probably built for horses."

"You were singing."

"I was singing patriotic songs." Chris Carroll smiled a beatific smile.

Lieutenant Rogers grimaced. "Just tell me one thing," he said. "Who is responsible for all the hell raising going on around here?"

"I presume you are referring to General Stuart," Chris Carroll said. "You know, if I were you, I wouldn't monkey around with him."

There was a whistle from beside the road.

"Hey, Lieutenant, Annapolis on the radio here."

Lieutenant Rogers walked over to the car.

"Rogers here," he said.

"How did things go out there?"

"We got a few of them."

"Who are they?"

"Playboys. The main one we got is that Chris Carroll. You know. The one we've had trouble with before. The one who's married to Pamela Hunt with all the money."

There was a clucking sound on the radio.

"Rogers, I hate to have to be the one to tell you, but I think you've got the wrong man. And while you were catching him, a thousand men were ripping up the Baltimore and Ohio Railroad at Sykesville."

"A thousand?"

"Yes, and they're not playboys either. Rogers, the governor has ordered out a full battalion of the National Guard to cope with this situation. Get over to Ellicott City right away and meet Colonel Flance, the commander. Tell him exactly what you know about these people."

9

—————

☆

June 29, 1863
Fitz Lee went off, under orders, to burn a
bridge at Sykesville. . . . The main force halted
to tear up the track where they struck it. . . .
It was time devouring work.

Douglas Southall Freeman,
Lee's Lieutenants—Vol. III

At six o'clock in the morning the last truck got
into line. Blackford sternly faced Mulcahy.

"Get in the wagon and start the engine," he said.

"But we been chopping trees and digging all
night," Mulcahy said. "We got to have some rest."

"Whatever you get you'll get when we catch up
with the general," Blackford said. "We're twenty
miles behind him now, I reckon."

Blackford waved his hand and the one hundred
and twenty-five guards climbed into the cabs. Their
horses had been taken on to the north when Colonel Chambliss and his men from the roadblock
passed by at a little after four o'clock.

"I still don't like it," Mulcahy grumbled, getting
into the cab. "I'm not only tired. I'm hungry."

Blackford cocked his pistol noisily.

The trip to Sykesville took slightly more than an hour. Blackford found General Stuart sitting his horse at the sound end of the bridge over the Patapsco River. The captain climbed down out of the truck and walked over.

"These wagons move right along when they've a mind to," he said.

The general nodded wearily and looked at his watch.

"Chambliss' men will finish crossing in less than an hour," he said. "We'll be in Westminster by three o'clock."

"Will General Lee be there, do you think?"

"Unless I'm mistaken, either Ewell or Early will be there." He pulled a map out of his blouse and spread it across his saddle and studied it, all the while pulling on his beard. "If we don't find either one in Westminster, I believe I'll move west from there. I've been looking at this town of Gettysburg. I don't know General Lee's timetable, but I calculate he ought to be between Chambersburg and Gettysburg tomorrow morning. We'll try there, anyway." He looked up from his map and frowned. "I declare," he said, "that man Mulcahy is the most persistent man I ever saw."

Blackford turned to see Mulcahy approaching.

"I got something legitimate to talk about this time," Mulcahy said, looking up at the general.

"Talk on," the general said, folding his map.

"I'm worried about this bridge," Mulcahy said. "Do you expect us to take these trucks across there?"

"I do."

"We can't do it. Look at that sign there on the end of the bridge. It says that loads of twenty thousand pounds are prohibited and that violators are subject to a fine of twenty-five bucks. There isn't a truck in this convoy with an axle load of less than fifteen tons. Aside from the fines, the whole thing is dangerous. That bridge is liable to collapse. It looks rickety to me."

General Stuart sighed and looked up at the sign.

"You have the first truck in line, Mr. Mulcahy?"

"I do."

"Then you will be kind enough to move it up close to the bridge and start unloading it. When you have lightened it enough to get it across, please let me know."

"Unload? Me? I'm a truck driver, not a ware-houseman. It would be against the union rules for me to unload."

"I don't give a damn about Union rules. We operate under Confederate rules. Unload it!"

Mulcahy drove his truck up close to the bridge and walked around to the rear where he began methodically unloading boxes. He was still unloading when the last horseman cleared the bridge.

"General," Blackford said, "he's the slowest mortal I ever did see. We may spend the rest of the afternoon just waiting for him to unload that wagon."

"I must admit he's pretty slow," the general said, looking at his watch with a sad expression, "but we shall see what we shall see."

It was eleven o'clock when Mulcahy stepped back and looked at the pile of boxes on the ground.

"I think I can get her across now," he said.

"Do it then," the general said.

The general walked his horse to the north side of the stream and waited. When the truck came crawling across the old iron span, he waved it to the side of the road.

"Now, Mr. Mulcahy," he said, "go back and carry all that material you unloaded across the bridge and load it back up again. And while you are across there you might have the next five wagons in line start unloading."

Mulcahy spat on the ground in disgust.

"You mean you expect me to carry all those boxes across that bridge, one by one?"

"I'm not at all concerned with how many boxes you carry at one time. The main thing is that you carry them across."

Mulcahy trudged back across the bridge and Blackford shook his head in disapproval.

"If all those drivers unload their wagons and

then carry those boxes across that bridge, General Lee is going to be in Boston before we catch up with him."

The general grinned, winked, and shook his head.

"I doubt if all those drivers will unload their wagons," he said. "They don't like to work any better than Mulcahy does." He pulled out his watch. "We ought to begin making up a little time soon." He pointed across the bridge where some of the truck drivers had come to talk to Mulcahy.

"Wilson," one of the drivers said, "we don't think you're very smart. Because of you and your ideas we spent all night chopping down trees and now you've got it fixed so we'll be carrying boxes across that bridge for the next two days. It just ain't going to work."

"The hell it ain't going to work," Mulcahy said. "You guys got to back me up. Remember our motto, 'In union there is strength.' Why do you suppose that old general has been yakking at us to hurry up for? Carrying these boxes will take up time and I don't think he's got time. He's going to have to let us go."

"You might think so, but the rest of us don't."

"Just look at him," Mulcahy said, gesturing wildly. "He's always pulling that watch out of his pocket. Or look at it another way. Even if he's not impatient, he's got two strikes on him. Sooner or later somebody's going to rescue us."

"Jimmy Hoffa, I suppose," a man said.

Mulcahy pointed at the sky.

"What do you think that is up there? It ain't no eagle. It's a helicopter. It's been up there for an hour. I'm telling you guys, people know where we are. If we can just stall long enough the state cops or the army will get us out of this jam. That's what I'm doing. Stalling."

"Mulcahy, that old bastard has got half the cops in Maryland handcuffed together in their own cruisers already. You're crazy. Anyway, we came to notify you that we elected a new road committee. As of now, you are an ex-chairman."

"What do you think *you're* going to do?"

"We're going to drive across that bridge."

"Supposing it collapses?"

"I don't suppose it's ever entered that bird brain of yours that if it does collapse, then all of us on this side of the bridge are free."

"Well, then, supposing it *doesn't* collapse?"

"Then we'll play ball with him. Maybe if we co-operate he'll go easier on us. Maybe he'll let us go."

The trucks took the bridge one at a time. As fast as they came off the rickety old iron structure, Blackford sent them on ahead to join the cavalry which had broken its camp on the north side of the stream and was moving out. Shortly after the last truck had cleared, Blackford allowed Mulcahy to turn his truck around to go back to the other side of the river to reload. The truck never reached the south side of the stream. As it neared the center of the span, there was a whistling noise followed by an explosion that sent a water spout high into the air. Mulcahy stopped his truck and opened the cab door and started to run to safety on the south shore, but the ten horsemen who had been sitting there thundered out onto the planks and swept him up in their rush to the north side.

"What the hell was that?" Mulcahy asked the general from his seat behind one of the cavalrymen.

"That was artillery, Mr. Mulcahy," the general said calmly. "I don't think this is any place for us." He nodded to the cavalrymen and they started to canter up the road. Mulcahy bounced around frantically on the horse's rump, trying to get off.

"My truck!" he yelled. "What about my truck?"

"Mr. Mulcahy, it's a mighty fine wagon and I hate to lose it, but my advice to you is to stay up there."

There was another whistling noise and an explosion and the truck began to smoke and burst into flames.

"They hit the fuel tank," Mulcahy said. "I'll get fired. Even the union can't help me."

Halfway up the hill, on the way out of Sykesville, the horses stopped and the men turned to look down at the town. They were just in time to see a whole barrage land in the river. The bridge slowly settled into the water.

For half an hour after leaving the hill the general, Blackford, and their escort cantered along a road to the west. They passed between the double column of cavalry which was moving steadily. They also passed the long line of trucks which had stopped once more.

"Now, what in blazes do you suppose has gone wrong?" the general said, making a wry face. He spurred his horse to a gallop.

When the general reached the head of the line of trucks he found the union negotiating committee standing in the middle of the road arguing with General Wade Hampton.

"I thought you fellows told me you were going to co-operate," General Stuart said, dismounting.

"That's what we're trying to do," one of the drivers said. "Just take a look at that road he wants us to go on. I swear, it goes straight up in the air."

"It *is* a pretty steep hill," General Hampton said, "but it shouldn't trouble them any. The engines on those wagons are strong enough to pull the loads up it."

"It will take two hours for all of our trucks to pull this hill in creeper," the driver said. "This road is an old abandoned mountain road and all the grades are just like this one. At the rate we can travel on it, we won't get to Westminster till midnight. I know an easier way to get there." He spread a road map on the ground and knelt down. "Look at this, General." He bent over and traced with his pencil. "Down here is a good, new road to Westminster. There are no steep grades and no sharp turns. We can do fifty or sixty miles an hour. At that rate all of us can be in Westminster in an hour and a half."

The general tugged on his beard and looked around.

"It will take us about nine miles out of our way," Blackford said. "Nine miles may not make any difference to the wagons, but it would to our horses. They're tired."

"We can take the trucks by the new road," the driver said. "Your horses can use the old one."

"Every time something like this comes up we lose another four hours," the general said skeptically. "How do I know this isn't another of your Yankee tricks?"

"You've got an armed guard in every cab now," the driver said. "You can double it if you want to. The thing is, we'll be in Westminster before you are."

The general looked around the group and pulled at his beard again, then knelt down to look closer at the map.

10

Colonel George Flance stood on the south bank of the Patapsco River and looked at the burning wreckage of the bridge, beating his trousers with his swagger stick.

"I don't see how that truck got on that bridge," he said. "All we had to do was put a new floor on it. Well, we'll have to do it the other way." He spread a map on the ground and got down on his knees. "The spotter says these horsemen have turned north on the old mountain road. The head of the column is right here." He made a big X for his staff to see. "That means they'll be in Westminster in two hours at the earliest. We'll circle west from here." He drew a long line on the map. "We'll get over on Route 27, which is a good concrete highway, and shoot straight into Westminster. It's thirty-seven miles and we can do it in an hour. That will give us plenty of time to set up a roadblock and get ready." He stood erect and strutted to his command car to issue his new orders. Within ten minutes the long convoy had turned around and was speeding west toward Route 27.

It was close to three in the afternoon when the lead jeep breasted a small knoll and rolled down to the intersection with Route 26. As it did so, a State Police cruiser, a trooper handcuffed to the wheel, came over the brow of the hill on the right. The men in the jeep couldn't see the pistol in the driver's side, but they could see that the cruiser's siren was blowing and that its red blinker was flashing. Behind it was a long line of commercial trucks. The jeep driver swung into the middle of the intersection and the sergeant in the rear seat nimbly hopped out onto the concrete, his hand upraised. The police cruiser ran right up to him and stopped. The back doors opened and two dirty, bewhiskered men climbed out to hold up *their* hands against the army convoy coming up from the south.

"Hey, there!" The captain, who was in the front seat of the jeep, jumped out to join his sergeant. "You can't do that!" he yelled.

"Son," one of the two bewhiskered men said, "we just happens to be in a hurry."

"Don't son me," the captain said. "I happen to be in a hurry, too, and I'm on *government* business."

"Government business?" The bearded man looked at the convoy and then turned to his companion. "Eben, can you make out the readin' on that there contraption they got yonder?" He pointed at a tank.

"I declare, Zeke, it says United States Army." He turned and made a hand signal toward the line of trucks.

"Say, young feller," Zeke asked the captain, "what might them things be with the long smokestacks stickin' out t' front on 'em?"

"They happen to be medium tanks."

"Do tell?" Zeke raised his eyebrows. "Tell them Yanks to climb down off the top of them medium tanks."

"I'll do no such thing."

The captain felt a hard object pressing his ribs.

"I'll just take that little peashooter you got there," Zeke said, reaching for the pistol in the captain's holster. "Now tell them Yanks to come down out of there and let's have a stop to this argifyin'."

"You wouldn't dare shoot an officer of the United States Army," the captain said.

"They's been officers of the United States Army gettin' shot 'most every day now for quite a long time. I don't mind tellin' you that I been baggin' my share."

Fifteen or twenty dirty, bearded, booted men had begun sauntering toward the intersection from the line of trucks, headed by a man in a slouched, plumed hat who wore a heavy mustache, a long saber, and a gray uniform.

"What's going on here?" the man asked.

"Hi ya, Cap'n Blackford," Zeke said. "We-uns are havin' a little trouble here. This is part of the Yank Army and I reckon they ought to surrender peaceably, but they have other ideas."

The captain looked over the situation.

"Zeke," he said, "you and Eben go over there and get those men off those perches. Be pleasant, but be firm. I imagine they'll give in without any trouble, but if they don't, you have my permission to shoot them."

The National Guard captain shrugged his shoulders.

"All right," he said, "you've got us. Never mind the rough stuff. They'll come down." He waved.

The men climbed down from the turrets and stood at the edge of the road. Zeke Carter wandered back up the column for thirty yards to where the first army truck was standing. A dozen soldiers were craning their necks out the side.

"What's going on over there?" one of them asked Zeke. "Why are you troopers arresting the captain?"

"He got uppity. He's right uncivil, that's what."

"All officers think they're little tin gods."

"Where you fellers aheadin' for?" Zeke asked.

"Westminster."

"Westminster? We're aheadin' that way, too. Tell you what we'll do for you fellers, seein's how we're all goin' to the same place. We'll let you come along with us. Now we ain't goin' to be movin' for a spell, so y'all can get out of them wagons and stretch your legs while I go along here and talk to these other Yanks. Jes' stack your arms over there aside the road and have yourselves a nice rest."

The army convoy was plainly visible to the drivers of the trucks that had come to a halt behind the cruiser. In one of the cabs Wilson Mulcahy sat morosely watching the scene. Suddenly he sat up and faced the driver next to him.

"Hey!" he said. "Our guards are gone."

"Sure. They went down the road there."

"Look where they went. What do you see?"

"Army trucks—and tanks."

"That's what I see. And they're *our* army, too. If we could make a quick break for it and run down along that army column, we'd get those soldiers between us and these hillbillies. We'd be protected."

"Maybe you got something there, Wilson."

"You're damned right I got something. Look, I'll take over this truck. You run back along the line and tell everybody to follow me when I pull out. Follow me, get it?"

As the word was being passed along the line,

Colonel Flance was sitting in *his* command car at the rear of the army convoy. He had a map spread out on his lap and was patiently going over the plans for the Westminster roadblock with his staff. Suddenly he looked up from his work and noticed that the convoy had stopped. He grabbed his radio microphone.

"Sagamore Forward!" he yelled into it. "This is Sagamore Six. Come in Sagamore Forward!"

There ensued a series of screeches and whistlings before a voice was heard.

"This here's that Sagamore Forward you been ayellin' for. What do you want?"

The colonel looked at the microphone unbelievingly.

"Why's the convoy stopped? What's the matter up there?" he finally said.

"That's a longish story. The main thing is we is stopped and it's likely to be a spell before we start again. If—" There was the sound of voices yelling and one suddenly boomed forth. "Hey, Zeke, them wagons is runnin' away."

The colonel poked his driver in the shoulder.

"Get up there! Quick!"

The staff car pulled out of line with squealing tires and streaked along the left-hand lane toward the head of the column. As it neared the top of the hill, a giant truck broke over the rise coming the other way. The chauffeur of the staff car looked and then yanked his steering wheel. The car veered sharply to the left, skidding out onto the shoulder in a cloud of dust. It ran along the shallow ditch, out of control for a moment, then bumped over the grass embankment to come to rest in a tangle of wire fencing. Mulcahy, in *his* attempt to avoid a collision, had also pulled to the left to hug the center line, causing the trailer to sway within inches of the army trucks that had been sitting quietly with engines idling. The army drivers acted instinctively. Most of them pulled *their* front wheels to the right and stepped on the gas. Trucks ended up at all angles and facing in all directions. To add to the confusion, soldiers scrambled for safety over the tailgates and through the rolled-up canvas at the sides. Some carried their rifles with them and some left their rifles in the trucks. On the other side of the road the truckers also were in a mess. Drivers had applied brakes to keep from hitting the trailers in front of them. Others had run along the shoulder. By the time they all came to a stop, they were badly disarranged. Within a period of sixty seconds the whole highway had become twisted and tangled. Practically all the vehicles of both columns were off the road, leaving the center of the highway open. And down the center, straddling the line, a jeep rolled slowly, followed by three tanks. Captain Blackford stood in the jeep beside Eben Raleigh. On top of the tanks were swarms of men. As the procession moved down the line, the men dropped off the tanks to cover the soldiers and the trucks.

Mulcahy had run back along the pavement to confront the occupants of the staff car as the jeep appeared.

"You skinny little louse," he shouted at the colonel, "what were you doing on the wrong side of the road? If it hadn't been for you, all of us would have got clear. Now some of these poor damned drivers are stuck with the Confederates."

"I reckon as how *all* you boys is stuck with the Confederates." Eben Raleigh reached over and extracted the pistol from the colonel's holster, then faced Mulcahy and shook his head. "As for you, Mr. Mulcahy, you're goin' to be aridin' the sharpest backed mule I can find."

"Give me back that pistol," the colonel said.

"Nope. You're surrendered. General Stuart's goin' to be mighty pleased to find we catched us a real live colonel of the United States Army. I don't recollect we catched a colonel for quite a spell." He turned to Blackford.

"I'll take charge of him," Blackford said.

"When the United States government learns you have interfered with the operations of this battalion, the whole army will be after you in force," the colonel said.

"Never you mind," Blackford said calmly. "The whole United States Army has been after us for quite a spell now and you can see that we're not one whit worried." He turned to Eben. "Eben, you better start straightening these wagons out. The last time they got themselves in a mess it took us five hours to get them going again."

It took until after dark before the convoy rolled into the outskirts of Westminster. General Stuart was sitting his horse, waiting.

"I'm sorry we took so long acomin', General," Eben Raleigh said, "but we run into a passel of trouble."

"I'm getting so I expect that with these wagons," the general said, "but I knew you'd get here."

"General, for once it warn't the wagons. We got ourselves a part of the Union Army." He turned and pointed at the staff car which had just driven up. The door opened and Blackford stepped out, then bent over to look inside.

"Come out of there, Colonel, and meet the general," Blackford said.

The colonel got out of the car, his face grim.

"General," Blackford said, "this is Colonel Flance of the Union Army."

"Colonel George B. Flance," the colonel said stiffly, "Maryland National Guard. May I know who I am addressing?"

"Stuart," General Stuart said. "General James E. B. Stuart, Confederate States of America."

"It is impossible that you could be General

Stuart, sir. You'd be one hundred and thirty years old."

"That's how old I feel," the general said. "It's been a hard ride." He looked the colonel up and down and rubbed his beard thoughtfully. "Well, Colonel, if you'll excuse me, I'll have to get on with things. I'll talk with you later." He turned to Blackford. "We're pretty well cleaned up here," he said. "Hampton tore up about two miles of the railroad and we've paroled all the prisoners into the custody of the town authorities. You can escort this column out the road to Union Mills, Captain."

"General, I think I ought to say a word about these wagon drivers," Blackford said.

"What about them?"

"I reckon we better give them a chance to sleep. They're pretty near tuckered out. On the way here six of them went to sleep while they were running along the road. Their wagons near upset."

"That means losing more time," the general said. "They've already cost us five hours this evening."

"I know it's mighty disappointing, General, but if we don't do something like that we're going to lose them all. Besides, this evening wasn't entirely their fault. We had those Yanks to contend with, too. And I can vouch for the fact that these wagons will move right along when they get the chance. They won't hold us up much."

The general sighed heavily.

"All right, Blackford," he said. "We'll let the drivers sleep for a time. Lord knows, our men can use some rest, too. Tell them to pull off to the side of the road after they've cleared the town here."

"Yes, sir."

"You can turn over your prisoners to the town authorities for parole."

11

The governor of the state of Maryland and the general commanding that state's National Guard were standing before a large wall map.

"The last report of our spotter plane placed the van of this force here at Union Mills," the general said, using a pointer to mark the spot.

"I don't care where they are," the governor said, scowling. "I just want you to do something. I'm tired of having all the law-enforcement agencies of this state made fools of by a little band of Confederate soldiers."

The general raised his eyebrows.

"You don't really believe they're Confederates?"

"All I know is that somebody is raising hell with

the chickens, pigs, railroads, and the people of this state. He claims he is Jeb Stuart. More than four hundred people who have seen him or talked to him claim he is Jeb Stuart."

"I can present proof from the War Department files that Jeb Stuart was killed at Yellow Tavern in 1864."

"I don't give a damn what the files say. The only thing we have to go on is that we are dealing with someone who claims he is Jeb Stuart. He's out-smarted everyone who has tried to deal with him in the last thirty-six hours. If it will help *you* any to deal with him, change *your* name to Phil Sheridan."

"Governor, there's no question about this. It's just part of the Gettysburg Centennial that has gotten out of hand."

"You're dead wrong," the governor said belliger-ently. "I've been on the telephone all day and I've talked to everybody from the chairman of the Civil War Centennial Commission up to and including the President. There is no formal centennial pageant celebrating the Battle of Gettysburg. As far as I've been able to determine they don't even intend to let Carl Sandburg read a poem."

"They don't?" The general's face went blank.

"No. Now what are you going to do about this?"

"I've already issued the orders. The 114th Regi-mental Combat Team is already assembling here at Silver Run. It will be in position no later than two o'clock this morning. It is on good defensive ground and it is athwart the road to Gettysburg."

"Suppose they attack before you are ready?"

"I have reason to believe they won't. They've gone into bivouac. They had to stop and rest sometime."

"I don't like this defensive business. That's what Flance was doing when we last heard from him. It didn't work at Roxbury Mills last night. I think we should attack."

"Governor, I have to get my troops in position to attack. This business tonight is designed to hold a line until I can get organized. At seven o'clock tomorrow morning I *will* attack."

12

———

June 29–30, 1863
During the night, scouts brought word that the enemy's cavalry was . . . to the northwest of Union Mills. Stuart directed [the march] toward Hanover, twelve miles north of Union Mills.

D. S. Freeman, *Lee's Lieutenants*—Vol. III

General Stuart was animated and chuckling to himself as he paced up and down under the big tree. He stopped and faced the little group of staff officers.

"Don't let your enthusiasm get the best of you," he told them. "While it's always a pleasure to outwit a Yankee, everyone has to be careful. There can be no mistakes here. Each man must do his part without any further instructions. It is now three o'clock in the morning. That means it is just two hours until daylight. In that two hours this whole force has got to move twelve miles. When Judson Kilpatrick launches his attack here in the morning, he mustn't find so much as a mule." He looked about him. "Hampton?"

"My men are already on the move. I estimate they are already halfway to Hanover."

"Chambliss," General Stuart said, "are these your troops moving by here now?"

"Yes, sir."

"Move them at a gallop." He turned to Blackford. "Now, Blackford, these wagon drivers have had six hours of sleep and there is no excuse for delay. You will move independently of everyone else. You are to destroy any wagon that does not keep up. I've instructed all commanders to leave the center of the road open to you so that you can move fast. Take the wagons right on into Hanover and wait there. Fitz Lee is moving directly from Westminster to Hanover and he will arrive in the town about eight o'clock. You will report to him when he arrives. There is a chance that we may turn west to Gettysburg if General Lee is there. However, if General Early or General Ewell has gone on north and east to Harrisburg, we will go there. Fitz Lee will know. Are you clear on what to do?"

"Yes, sir."

"Godspeed and good luck, gentlemen. You may mount up."

13

The radio in the command tent squawked insistently. The sergeant made a wry face and looked nervously over his shoulder at the general.

"Sagebrush to Sagebrush Spot," the general said. "Sagebrush calling Sagebrush Spot. Come in, Sagebrush Spot. We want to know where those horses are. Where are they?"

"Keep your shirt on, Sagebrush," a voice said over the loudspeaker. "I'm looking for them. I don't see a thing right now."

"You must be looking in the wrong place."

"I'm right over U.S. 140 and Old Hanover Road."

"They were there last night."

"I know they were there last night. I was the guy that found them for you."

"They were there at two o'clock this morning. One of our patrols ran into them there."

"What does your patrol say now, if it's so damned good?"

"The patrol was captured. We haven't heard from it since. Look around. They must be someplace near there."

"I'll go up higher and look around."

The sergeant sat patiently in his chair for ten minutes. The general paced up and down.

"Sagebrush Spot to Sagebrush," the radio shouted. "Sagebrush Spot to Sagebrush! I'm at five thousand feet and looking. I've found your cowboys."

The general took two strides across the tent and grabbed the microphone.

"Stop being funny and give us some co-ordinates!" he yelled. "And be damned quick about it. The artillery is waiting."

"The artillery is out of luck, Sagebrush."

"What do you mean—out of luck?"

"Because these horses are all in Pennsylvania. Every last one of them has crossed the state line."

"What difference does that make? We can still reach them with our heavies."

"We're the *Maryland* National Guard, remember? You can't go shooting up Pennsylvania. You want to start a war between the states?"

The governor of Pennsylvania had been asleep when the call came from Maryland and he was still sitting on the edge of his bed in his pajamas.

"I know it's serious, Governor," he said into the phone. "And I have no intention of taking any half measures. I've already alerted the State Police *and* the National Guard."

"Look, Governor," the governor of Maryland said, "there's one thing you'd better do right away. Unless I'm mistaken, the Hanover breeding farm is right in the path of these people. If they ever get onto that farm there won't be another trotting or pacing race in the country for the next five years. As the governor of a state that depends on trotting races for a lot of its income, I implore you to call that farm and have him get his stock out of the way. I'm sure the governor of New York would concur with me."

"I'll take care of it at once."

The governor of Pennsylvania hung up the phone, then picked it up again and put in the call to Hanover.

"I want you to act and act fast," he told the manager of the breeding farm. "If you look out your window you'll probably see a lot of men on horseback. These men are posing as Confederates. In reality they are horse thieves."

"Who are they posing as?"

"Confederate cavalry. I know it sounds crazy, but you'll just have to take my word for it and do as I tell you and not ask questions. Get your handlers to move every head of stock you have. I don't care what you do with them or where you take them, but get them as far away from Hanover as you can."

"Most of our stock is in the back pastures," the manager said. "I'll get at it right away." He turned from the phone and buzzed the barns and range houses on the intercom. "How many head do we have in the corrals?" he asked.

"About a hundred, mostly foals and brood mares," the range boss said.

"All right, we'll have to forget *them*. Take everything else on the farm and get them out of here as fast as you can. Use every available man and get moving."

"You mean you just want us to drive them off?"

"That's right."

"What's up? Somebody drop an atom bomb?"

"It's the Confederates."

"What are the Confederates doing with an atom bomb?"

"Don't ask questions. Get a move on."

"Okay, boss. Where do we go?"

"What's the best road to get out on?"

"From the back pastures it would be the old Hunterstown Road that goes up through the mountains and comes back in on the other side of Gettysburg. We can take them that way."

"Okay. I'll have the boys up here at the house go and lock all the corral gates that aren't already locked. It will take a long time to break three hundred and fifty padlocks. That ought to give you time to get away."

The manager called the governor back at seven o'clock and reported that everything was under control at the farm. The governor was still in his pajamas and had been joined by his superintendent of State Police. After completing the phone call he went back to the map that had been spread out on his bedroom floor.

"I figure you have two hours to get your men assembled," he told the superintendent. "But don't forget what happened in Maryland."

"We're rendezvousing east of town," the superintendent said. "I won't send a man in there until I've made a complete reconnaissance. They won't get any of my men."

"Keep me informed. I'll let you know by radio as soon as the Guard is assembled and ready to go."

14

June 30, 1863
The mules were wild with hunger and thirst . . .
the procession ground to a halt.
Burke Davis, *Jeb Stuart, The Last Cavalier*

General Stuart rode up to the fences of the breeding farm at seven-thirty. Wade Hampton, dismounted, was directing a large number of dismounted cavalrymen. They seemed to be tearing the boards off the gates or hammering away at locks. General Stuart got off his horse and climbed a fence.

"What's going on here, Wade?" he asked.

"There must be more than three hundred enclosures here. Every damned gate has been locked."

"Just what purpose did you have in mind?"

"There are fifteen hundred head of stock on this farm. That's enough to furnish remounts for every one of my men. I mean to have them."

"How many men do you have in here?"

"The 1st and 2nd North Carolina."

"Wade, far be it from me to question you, but I think I should point out that you have two full regiments of cavalry penned up here where they can't get out in a hurry. In view of the fact that the Yankees are only seven miles away, I suggest you recall them. I appreciate your need for re—"

General Hampton was staring over General Stuart's shoulder in dismay. General Stuart turned to see Captain Blackford get out of a police cruiser, accompanied by five of the truck drivers.

"That'll be more trouble," General Hampton said.

Blackford came up and saluted.

"We've been back and forth by this place three times without seeing you," he said. "If it hadn't been for that plume in your hat, I might never have noticed you. I'd have sworn y'all were working on this farm."

"You found us," the general said. "What is it?"

"The wagons are low on fuel. The drivers say they can't go any further on what they have."

"Where do you get more fuel?"

"At places called gas stations."

"How long will it take?"

"Two or three hours. There are a hundred wagons."

A soldier came running up to the group. General Hampton nodded at him.

"We got through to the other end of them corrals," the soldier said, "but the horses have all been druv off. They got 'bout an hour's head start."

"We can't catch them," Hampton said. "Call in the men." He turned to General Stuart. "If I were you, Jeb, I'd give up on those wagons, too. We can't stay here three hours."

"I'd hate to give up on them now," General Stuart said, and pulled on his beard. Suddenly his face lighted up. "I'm beginning to get an idea. This is a horse farm with no horses on it. We'll put horses on it. Blackford, go back into Hanover and refuel those wagons. Do it as fast as you can. In the meantime, I want you to send every horseman in town back out here to the farm. You can send that carriage of yours down toward Westminster to intercept Fitz Lee. Tell him not to enter Hanover at all. He is to circle the town and come here."

The general turned to Wade Hampton.

"Now, Wade, we'll start making this farm look more natural. If Blackford drove by here three times without recognizing us, then Judson Kilpatrick isn't going to find any Reb cavalry either. I want every soldier and horse in this command put out in the back pastures. Have the men dismount, unsaddle, and carry their gear off into the woods and stay out of sight. Now, do you have any men that can talk Yankee talk?"

"I reckon I have a few."

"Find some farmer's clothes and put them out here with rakes and shovels like they were working. If old Judson rides up here they can send him on a wild-goose chase. Just to be safe, have a few of your men nail these corrals shut again. In case our actors don't fool anybody, we'll catch Judson while he's trying to get through the fences."

It was eight-thirty before the first line of trucks came rolling into the Keystone Esso filling station in Hanover to stop in front of a diesel oil pump.

"Fill 'er up," the driver said, and waited while the attendant put oil into the tank.

"That'll be thirty dollars and twenty cents, please," the attendant said.

The driver reached into his pocket and extracted a credit card, handing it down to the man on the ground.

"How do you expect to get fuel in an Esso station with a Shell credit card?" the attendant asked.

"I never thought about it until this minute. Zeke, here, said to drive in, so I drove in."

"Start thinking, sonny boy. I want my money."

"Zeke," the driver said, "we're in trouble. He won't take my credit card."

"Let me see it," Zeke said. He took it and turned it over and over. "Looks all right to me. I cain't read very good. What's the matter with it?"

"You have to have an Esso card," the attendant said. "That's a Shell card."

"Any of them other drivers got the right kind?"

"I don't know. I suppose so."

Zeke walked back along the line of trucks.

"You got one of these here credit cards?" he asked the driver of the second truck.

"Sure," the man said, handing down his card.

"What kind is it?"

"It's an Esso card."

"Then what are we awaitin' for?" Zeke asked. He turned, walked back, and thrust the card at the attendant. As the attendant looked at the card, the driver to whom it belonged rushed up and snatched it away.

"That's valuable," he said.

"We warn't goin' to harm it none," Zeke said.

"Zeke, how long do you think I'd last on this job if my boss found out I'd been charging other guys' fuel oil on this credit card. It's dishonest."

"If you paid for this other feller's fuel with your card and he paid for your fuel with his'n, it would make things sort of even, wouldn't it?"

"I guess so."

"Then that's how we're agoin' to do it." Zeke shouted down the line. "All you other fellers get back in your wagons. We're agoin' to look for a Shell place."

The convoy rolled out into the street, around a

block, and back to the town square. A medium tank appeared at the head of a column coming from the other direction. Zeke held up his hand.

"Eben," he yelled, "are you in that contraption?"

"Here I be," Eben said, popping out of the turret.

"Eben, I don' know why you got to go ridin' round in that thing all the time. Whyn't you ride in one of these here wagons like the rest of us?"

" 'Cause I just happen to enjoy this here tank wagon. It's diff'rent. Besides, these Yanks in here are pretty good fellers. They ain't makin' no big thing about belongin' to the Union all the time."

"Eben, what I want to know is, have you seen one of them Shell places?"

"That's funny you'd ask me, Zeke. I jes' come from one. I'm lookin' for a Gulf place myself."

15

The governor of Pennsylvania and the commanding general of *his* National Guard stood before the radio. The general was talking to the pilot of the helicopter.

"Have you found those horses?"

"Yes, sir. Three big bunches of them. The biggest bunch is at the horse farm. They're—"

"I don't care anything about the horses at the breeding farm. If they're still there and haven't been stolen, that's all to the good. What about the others?"

"Well, there's a big bunch about five miles north and west of here. They're moving in the general direction of Gettysburg by way of Hunterstown.

Then there's a third bunch about two miles south of Hanover. They're riding across the fields to the northwest. It looks to me like they're purposely skirting the city."

"Do you see any horses in Hanover?"

"No, sir. Not a one."

The general tapped his forehead with his fingers. The governor looked at him anxiously.

"What do you think, General?"

"They're headed for Gettysburg, all right. Where else is there anything that would have any meaning to a group that is supposed to be Confederates?"

"Can you get your men there in time?"

"I don't care who gets there first. I think I know that ground better than anyone who calls himself Jeb Stuart. I've walked every foot of it since I was a boy."

"It's your baby." The governor smiled grimly and the general snapped the button on the radio microphone.

"Spotter, I want you to stay with the van of that column at all times. Don't let them out of your sight and report to me every ten minutes."

"Yes, sir. How about that other bunch behind?"

"Forget about them for the time being. If we get the first bunch, the second bunch will fall into our hands. Over and out." The general looked at the governor. "I think that before I go we ought to decide what to do about Hanover."

"Let's check with the police. The superintendent is on the spot there now." The governor nodded to his operator to switch radio channels. "Where are you now and what do you know of the situation in Hanover, Superintendent?"

"Hello, Governor. I'm at the road junction near the airport, which we control. That's three miles outside of town to the north. Things are a mess in Hanover."

"What's the trouble?"

"Basically, it's a traffic jam, the damnedest one I ever saw in my life. I'm just preparing to send a traffic detail of twenty-five men in there to get things moving."

"Are you sure it's safe to send your men in there?"

"Yes, sir. From what I've been able to learn there are no horses or horsemen in there now. There were quite a few of them in there earlier, but they've all been gone for some time."

"What's the cause of this traffic jam?"

"Trucks. Evidently when they came into town early this morning, the Confederates lined up every truck they could get their hands on and used them as sort of movable roadblocks. Anyway, now there are more than one hundred of these trucks lined up in various parts of town, clogging the main streets and blocking the side streets. It would have taken a traffic engineer in reverse to figure this thing out, but they seem to have done it with no effort at all. And the worst thing is, every time some of these trucks try to move around, as they seem to be doing, it gets worse."

"We're prepared to send some of the National Guard to Hanover on their way to Gettysburg. Do you need them?"

"No, sir. No, sir. You'd better keep them out of here, Governor. I'd hate to try and steer a convoy through this mess. Except for the traffic jam, things are all right here, anyway."

"All right. We'll issue new orders. You keep your twenty-five-man traffic detail there to clean up the place and send all the rest of your men to Gettysburg. That's where the real trouble is going to be."

16

☆

June 30–July 1, 1863
A punishing night march began. . . . New prisoners had been taken. . . . Fitz Lee, probing eastward towards York, discovered that General Early had left that town. . . . Stuart pushed the column towards Carlisle.

Burke Davis, *Jeb Stuart, The Last Cavalier*

A column of trucks headed by Captain Blackford had arrived at the Hanover Mobilgas station at the same time as another column headed by Eben Raleigh.

"This is the third time I been back here," Eben said. "Last time I come here I run into Gil Yancey. So far I only got me seven trucks refueled."

"Yes," Blackford said, shaking his head, "we've got to change our tactics. Eben, you take that tank wagon and go round everybody up. We're going to put all the Esso wagons in one line and all the Mobilgas wagons in another and stop this infernal running around. Now—"

A car came sliding up to the curb in front of the gas station and a man got out.

"Hey, there!" the man yelled from the street. "Are you men the drivers of these trucks that are blocking traffic here?"

"Who might that be?" Eben asked the drivers.

"That's a state trooper."

"Damnation! I thought we had all them varmints rounded up," Eben said. "He don't look like them other ones we caught."

"This one's a Pennsylvania state trooper. The ones you've been catching are Maryland state troopers."

"Damnation again!" Eben started walking slowly toward the state trooper, who eyed him suspiciously a moment and drew his pistol.

"Just stop where you are," the trooper said.

There was a loud report and the trooper's pistol spun from his hand. A soldier standing on the running board of one of the trucks looked admiringly at an M-1 rifle.

"I'll be doggoned," the soldier said. "This here Yank rifle is pretty good. I think I'll take it back home to use when I go a squirrel huntin'."

It was only a little more than an hour later when Sergeant Agnew, the head of the traffic detail, was led around in back of the Amoco Service Center to find his twenty-four troopers sitting lined up against the wall, handcuffed together. One of them looked up at the sergeant.

"Say, Sergeant," he said, "whatever became of

those guys on horseback we were supposed to watch out for?"

It was nearing dusk when General Stuart came out onto the porch of the manager's house at the breeding farm. He had pulled on his gloves and carried his hat in his hand.

"Blackford," he said, "you may have the buglers sound the call. It's time we were moving."

He walked over to where a group of officers were kneeling around a map that was spread out on the floor.

"You'll hurt your eyes in this light, gentlemen."

"Seems like we're goin' out of our way in order to get to York, General."

"Of course, it's out of our way," the general said. "Everything's out of our way. If we hadn't had to wait so long for these wagons, we'd be going west to Gettysburg instead of northeast to York." He turned and patted Blackford on the back. "I didn't mean to cast any aspersions on you, my friend. No one could have done any better than you with these stubborn wagon drivers. But I'm just as stubborn as they are." He turned to kneel by the map. "Having lost almost a whole day, gentlemen, we'll have to catch Ewell or Early at another place. They must be well north of here by now. As long as we're going north, we might just as well hit the Yanks where it hurts. Hanover Junction is the place. We'll tear up the railroad there and destroy the telegraph relay." He got to his feet. "Hampton, you do the dirty work and when you drop out of line to do it, Fitz Lee will take over the advance. And Wade, don't forget what I told you about skirting towns. I imagine a lot of people will be trying to find us by now. The less people that see us the better." He turned to Blackford. "Come along, Blackford. It will be good to have you riding with me again."

"General," Blackford said, as they walked down the steps to the horses, "I think you ought to try one of those carriages. They're right comfortable."

"Me? Cooped up in one of those things where I couldn't use my sword if I had to?" He patted his long saber and shook his head. "I'm a fighting general, Blackford."

It was six o'clock of a bright summer morning and a rider came galloping wildly along a road north and west of York, Pennsylvania. He approached a group of horsemen.

"General," he said, "Pink Coulter said I should fetch you right off."

"And who is Pink Coulter?"

"He's my sergeant. We're in the 13th Virginia. Me and the other fellers was out lookin' for General Early and we come to this sign aside the road. Cain't none of us read, but Pink Coulter can so he reads it and the first think he done was to send me skedaddlin' after you."

The general nodded to Blackford and the two of them spurred ahead after the rider. After a few minutes they came to a small group of men squatted in a circle on their haunches, holding the reins of their horses, talking, and chewing tobacco. One of them rose to his feet and came over.

"I'm Sergeant Coulter, sir," he said. "The sign's over yonder." He led the way to it and began reading aloud. " 'Pennsylvania Historical Marker. June 28, 1863.' " He stopped, spit out some tobacco juice, and looked up. "That's three days ago, ain't it, General?"

"That's right," the general said.

"Well, here's the rest of it. 'General Jubal Early's Confederates approached York by this route. Here Early sent Colonel French to York Haven to burn the bridges. He was ordered the next day to rejoin Lee's Army. Early returned over this road on June 30th.' That's jes' yestiddy, General. I don' know jes' where General Early returned to, but one thing's certain. He ain't here. He's done been here and gone."

"Sergeant, which way do you think he went?"

"General, they's four ways he could have gone. We know he didn't go south or we would have passed him. We know he didn't go east because that wouldn't have been returnin'. So he must have gone west or north. I rode along this here road to the west and it sure don't look to me like no army went thataway yestiddy. They ain't even no footmarks aside the road. I reckon General Early done gone north."

"What's the name of this place?"

"Near as I can make out, this here four corners is called Weigelstown. I don't rightly know where Weigelstown is, but that's where we be."

The general took out his map and turned to Blackford.

"We'll go northwest. I imagine Early is heading for Carlisle. We ought to catch up with him by midnight."

17

☆

The governor of Pennsylvania sat in the executive offices of the state capitol and looked first at the telegram in his hands and then up at the general and the pilot.

"Well, we know which direction they're headed," he said. "They sure raised hell with Hanover Junction. The railroad torn up, the depot burned down, the telephone and telegraph lines gone—"

"But why Hanover Junction?" the general asked. "It's hardly a dot on the map. It's been a ghost town for sixty years or more."

"General, I'm ashamed of you," the governor said. "You're not up on the state's history. In 1863 Hanover Junction just happened to be one of the

most important spots in the state of Pennsylvania."
He shook his head and turned to the pilot. "You'd
better use it as a hub for your search."

"Yes, sir."

"And this time, get the right horses."

The pilot flushed.

"I beg your pardon, Governor, but I still insist
that wasn't my fault. The general said not to let
those horses out of my sight and I didn't."

"But you ought to have been able to tell they
didn't have any riders on them," the general said.

"The ones back at the horse farm didn't have any
riders on them either."

The governor got up and walked to the wall map.
He inscribed a big circle with his hands.

"If you see any horses in this area, they're the
ones we want. And I want a full report this time.
There must be more than a thousand of them.
Maryland was all wrong on that. And I want to
know if those trucks are actually a part of this.
Count them if they are."

"Yes, sir."

The pilot found his first horseman at eight-
thirty .

"They're on Route 74 between Wellsville and
Dover," he told the governor. "They'll be in Carlisle before night."

"Good work. I'll start things moving at once."

"You better not act too fast, Governor. You better

wait to hear the rest.There are close to three thousand of them."

"Three thousand? Are you sure?"

"Yes, sir. And that isn't all. They got tanks. And those trucks. There's a hundred and twenty-five of them. If they happened to be loaded with men, that means another five thousand of them."

"Why, that's an army!" the governor said.

"I'll say it's an army."

"Maybe I'd better call the President. This looks like a Federal matter."

"Yes, sir. That's what I'd do. And, Governor—"

"Yes?"

"After I called the President, I'd start running. If they turn right at Wellsville, it's only fourteen miles to where you're sitting."

18

☆

> In the late afternoon of July 1, when the thin
> van . . . reached Carlisle . . . the weary troopers
> scarcely were in condition to clear the place. . . .
> Stuart had with him few men at the time . . .
> but briskly he had Fitz Lee send in a flag of
> truce to demand the surrender. . . . He began a
> slow shelling with a battery. . . . Afterward, some
> of the men scarcely knew whether they actually
> had bombarded the town or merely threatened
> to do so. . . . A cavalry barracks was burned, but
> no other buildings were set afire.
>
> **D. S. Freeman,** *Lee's Lieutenants*—Vol. III

General Stuart gazed down the heavily shaded
street.

"I came here, once, when I was just out of West
Point," he said. "It doesn't look the same."

"I don't like the looks of it either," Fitz Lee said.
"Maybe we should burn the place down."

The general turned to Blackford.

"Take a flag of truce and call upon the commander of the army post," he said. "You may
present him with my demand for his surrender.
You might look around for signs, too. General Early
seems to have developed a penchant for keeping
me informed in that manner." He watched Blackford ride off and turned back to Fitz Lee. "If we're

going to capture this army post, I think we ought to try out those tank wagons. Get them on the radio machine."

The tanks came rumbling up the road and Eben Raleigh poked his head out the turret.

"Eben," the general said, "can those things shoot?"

"These fellers say they can."

"We may have to use them."

"I don't reckon's how I know how to work them."

"You'll have to learn, then. We'll do a little harmless shooting and you and the men in the other wagons watch exactly how it's done. Don't miss a thing."

Eben ducked down into the tank.

"You heard the general. We better get started."

The sergeant picked up the microphone.

"Hotbox Leader to Hotbox Two and Three. Opportunity knocks. Do you read me?"

"We sure do, Hotbox Leader."

"On command, then, load and fire three. Eartay Asgay."

"Roger."

"Don't forget the Asgay Askmays."

"You Yanks sure do talk funny over them radio machines," Eben said. "I cain't make head nor tail of it."

"Never mind, Eben."

"You fellers mind if I try it?"

"Go ahead."

"This here's Hotbox Eben. You Hotbox Rebs watch them Yanks pretty close. 'Member exactly what they do 'cause when they get done shootin' these things, you got to do it."

Eben turned back to the tank crew.

"What's them things you're puttin' on your heads?"

"These are hoods. We put them on to sight with."

"I'll be doggoned. You mean you cain't shoot one of these here tank wagons without one of them hoods?"

"I'm afraid that's right."

"Seems to me it don't make much sense, but I guess you fellers know what you're adoin'."

The sergeant slowly brought his gun to bear.

"Hotbox Leader to Hotbox Two and Three. That oak tree is the target. Fire three rounds and prepare to scramble."

"Roger."

"Fire!" the sergeant said.

General Stuart's voice could be heard outside.

"These Yanks aren't very good shots, Fitz. I think you and I ought to have a little shooting match between us and show them how it's done." He banged on the tank. "Open up, Eben."

Eben turned to the sergeant.

"You fellers give me them hoods. We'll be needin' them to shoot with."

The sergeant shook his head vehemently as the sound of spurs could be heard on top of the tank.

"I'm coming down, Eben," General Stuart said, and stuck his head in to look around. "You having trouble?"

"Sometimes these Yanks won't do nothin' without a gun in their backs." Eben took the masks as they were handed to him. "You put these here hoods on like this, General," he said, trying to demonstrate. "Doggone. These hoods don't seem to fit worth a darn."

The general was struggling with his mask.

"It's the beard, Eben. It's the beard."

"General, we ain't goin' to be able to shoot without—" He stopped and held up his head. "My eyes is hurtin' somethin' terrible." He turned to look at the crewmen. "You fellers know anything about this?" He stopped and squinted. "Why, you fellers is bawlin' like babies."

"It's the tear gas," the sergeant gasped. "We got to get out of here."

"Jes' don' sit there doin' nothin'. If we got to git out of here, git to gittin'."

"But I can't see to drive."

"Drive it anyway. This thing will go anyplace. I seen it." Eben grabbed the microphone. "You fellers in them other Hotboxes foller us."

The tank began to roll forward. It lumbered down into a ditch and out again, wallowed through some high shrubs, and bulled its way through a chain-link fence that surrounded Carlisle Barracks. The other two tanks followed uncertainly and behind them came a little procession of horsemen. Inside the lead tank the sergeant peered half blindly, saw a building looming up, and flipped his vehicle to the right. The tank clattered noisily out onto a parade ground where men began scattering in all directions. It rattled between two houses, crossed a well-kept lawn, clipped a porch off another house, and crashed into a small wooden building that jutted out behind post headquarters. The building hardly slowed it down. It moved inexorably across the common in front of the administration building and rolled under the pillars that marked the main gate. Within ten minutes of the time it entered the post, the entire armored force of the Confederate States of America had swept out again to disappear in the city streets. When the tanks finally ground to a halt the first man to emerge from the turret was General Stuart. He was perspiring profusely and stopped to wipe his face with a huge handkerchief.

"I don't think these tank wagons will ever amount to much," he said to Fitz Lee. "They wouldn't be any good in a fight. No one can see anything. And if they had to go very far every man in them would be brainless from banging his head against the iron sides." He stopped to look up at Blackford, who came galloping around a corner on his horse. "Well, Blackford," he asked, "did you see the post commander?"

"Yes, sir."

"And what answer did you receive?"

" 'Nuts,' " Blackford said.

" 'Nuts'?" The general cocked his head. "What kind of an answer is that?"

"I don't rightly know, sir, but I took it to mean that he won't surrender." He pulled a slip of paper from his pocket. "On the way back here I found a sign. I copied it down."

"What does it say?"

"It says: 'General J. E. B. Stuart's Southern Cavalry arrived July 1st, 1863, by Dover and Dillsburg. Finding Ewell had left the day before, Stuart burned the U.S. Barracks and left for Gettysburg where the battle had begun.' "

"Battle? What battle? Isn't there—?"

There was a sound of a siren blowing and a Maryland State Police cruiser skidded around a corner and slid to a stop. Zeke Carter crawled out of the back seat.

"General," Zeke said, "I been followin' where you been in them tank wagons and I can tell you, you cut quite a swath. You set a buildin' on fire."

"Me? How?"

"You run right through it. It was the general's gym and steam room, whatever they are. You tipped over a stove and it set the buildin' on fire."

"Now, how do you suppose Ewell knew that?" the general asked thoughtfully.

"Knew what?"

"That we were going to set fire to a Yankee barracks." He walked over to his horse, mounted, and looked down. "Mount up, gentlemen," he said. "We'd better get to Gettysburg like he says."

19

★

July 2, 1863

Most of [our men] suffering an agony for sleep lay on the road with bridles in hand, some on rocks, and others on the wet earth, slumbering soundly. . . . Rest was brief. The men were shaken or aroused by shouts and were marched onward till flesh could stand no more.

Colonel R. L. T. Beale—9th Va. Cav.

General Stuart stood in the early-morning light on the fringe of a woods and looked up a hill. Just over the crest of that hill was the town of Gettysburg. He took the watch from his pocket, looked at it, and shook his head sadly.

"Blackford," he said, "tell the buglers to sound the call. I've given them all the rest I can."

As the bugles blew loud and clear on the morning air, the general strode wearily to his horse and mounted. In a moment, Blackford was back and looking up at him.

"I'm sorry, General," he said, "but I just saw that Union negotiating committee heading this way. I think it was a mistake to have let Mulcahy off that mule."

The general turned his horse to look down into the woods. The committee arrived in a V formation. Mulcahy stopped, planted his feet wide apart, folded his arms, and stuck out his chin.

"General," he said, "we're not going another foot."

The general smiled.

"You could have saved your breath, Mr. Mulcahy. You and the other drivers are free."

"Free?" Mulcahy's mouth dropped open.

"That's exactly what I said." The general nodded to Blackford to mount, turned his horse away, and started slowly up the hill. Blackford caught up with him just as they reached the crest. They both turned to look back.

"After all this work we went to, it seems a shame to let those wagons go," Blackford said, and sighed.

The general grinned and reached over and patted Blackford on the arm. Then he laughed aloud.

"Blackford, down there in Maryland these fellows drove off on a side road and it took them all night to get themselves dug out of that woods. Remember?"

"Yes, sir."

"They got themselves into that mess. *I* got them into this one. It was my idea that they drive off into this woods to do their resting. They'll still be digging and cutting and swearing when General Lee comes for them."

Blackford looked down at Mulcahy again. The truck driver was still standing with his arms folded and his legs planted wide apart. Blackford threw back his head and laughed. The general reached in his blouse and pulled out a cigar. He handed it to his adjutant.

"I don't smoke myself," he said, "but Eben Raleigh brought this to me. Light up. You probably won't be able to use them where we're going." He lit a match and Blackford puffed. Then both men turned their horses and rode over the hill.

hill is a farmhouse and a couple of barns. There's a truck coming out of the driveway of that farm and turning toward you, but, by God, there are no horses. Maybe what you need is an Indian scout."

The general looked up the road to see a truck, ancient and dilapidated, come into view. He waved his hand and the driver stopped and stuck his head out the window.

"Do you live on the other side of that hill?"

"Sure do."

"You been at home all morning?"

"Sure have."

"Did you see a column of horsemen come over that hill in the last hour?"

"Nope."

"My God, man, you must have. They rode right across your farm, three thousand of them."

The farmer shook his head emphatically.

"You must be crazy in the head. I been working out in back of the barn since daylight, loading this truck with feed. I never saw no horses. I haven't seen a horse in ten years, not on my farm anyway. I use a tractor myself."

The general looked at the farmer and then back at the truck drivers. He scowled for a moment and then ducked down into the turret. When he reappeared he had a submachine gun in his hands. He leveled it at the drivers.

"Just don't try any funny stuff," he said.

"Now, what is that for?" Mulcahy asked him.

"I'm not sure yet, but you can consider yourselves prisoners. Hurry up and get that truck dug out of there. We'll just take you along and find out what happened to those three thousand horsemen."

"How the hell would we know?"

"Anybody that knows that General Stuart abandoned three medium tanks must know what he did with three thousand horsemen. Now get to digging."

One of the men threw his hat down in disgust.

"God damn it!" he said. "Here we go again."

HEADQUARTERS
ARMY OF NORTHERN VIRGINIA

3 July, 1963

OWN LOSSES: None.

ENEMY LOSSES: None.

DAMAGE INFLICTED: Appropriated following items:

3722	chickens
346	pigs
79	beef cows
417	horses
194	cases spirits.

Destroyed:

1	bridge
1	depot

1   gymnasium and
               steam bath (?)
16   miles railroad.

RESULTS: None.

RECOMMENDATIONS: Let them bugle.

Signed/J. E. B. Stuart
Chief of Cavalry

STUART'S
GETTYSBURG
CAMPAIGN

JUNE, JULY
1963

PENNSYLVANIA

MARYLAND

HARRISBURG

Susquehanna River

Carlisle

74

Wellsville

15

34

Hill
16069242

GETTYSBURG

140

YORK

Dover

Weigelstown

30

Hunterstown

Hanover

GAS

Silver
Run

Union

Hanover
Junction